DEAD LAKE

DARCY COATES

For Em, Mandy, Fran and Steph.

Thank you.

CONTENTS

CHAPTER 1

Sam's breath caught as she stepped back from the car, jacket in one hand and a luggage bag in the other, and turned to face the densely wooded hills behind her. The strangest sensation had crawled over her, as if she were being watched.

That was impossible, of course. The lakeside cabin was the furthest from civilisation Sam had ever been. Nestled deep in Harob Forest and situated at the edge of a large lake, her uncle's property was a two-hour drive from the nearest town. Her Uncle Peter had said hiking paths snaked through the forest, but only a couple of them came near his part of the lake, and they weren't used often.

Despite that, Sam couldn't stop herself from running her eyes over the dense pine trees and shrubs that grew along the rocky incline. Only a colony of birds fluttering around a nearby conifer and the steady drone of insects broke the silence.

Sam turned back to the two-story cabin. The sun caught on the rough-hewn wood, making it almost seem to glow. It sat as close to the water as it could without compromising its foundations, and a balcony overlooked the lake. The rocky embankment rising behind it merged directly into the mountains, which grew more than a kilometre into the sky.

Peter had built the cabin nearly a decade before as a hobby to keep himself occupied on the weekends. He was proud of it, and rightfully so; Sam knew Peter made his living as a woodworker, but she hadn't expected him to be so proficient at it. The cabin looked as natural as the rocks, as though it could have sprouted out of the ground fully formed.

Sam shifted the luggage bag to her left hand and approached the front door. Her key fit into the lock and turned easily, and a grin grew across her face as the door creaked open.

The cabin's lower level was a single large room. A fireplace sat to her right; a stack of kindling waited for her near the soot-blackened hole, with a bracket holding aged firewood and an axe beside it. Two stuffed armchairs stood on thick animal furs, facing the fireplace. A polished wood table and chairs sat to Sam's left, near the kitchenette that took up the back part of the room. A stairway above the kitchen led to the upper level.

Sam dropped her bag beside the open door and marvelled at how clean the room was. Peter said he visited it at least once a month, and he must have been scrupulous with its maintenance. Sam felt in her jacket pocket for the letter he'd given her then unfolded it to re-read the characteristically abrupt chicken-scratch scrawl.

Sammy,

Have fun at the cabin. Don't get eaten by bears.

The lake's good for swimming. There's a canoe in the shed. And dry wood. Light a fire when the sun goes down—it gets cold at night.

There's no electricity or phone reception, so don't get into trouble, but if you do, there's a two-way radio in the kitchen cupboard. I wrote the most important codes beside it.

Don't go on the dock. (This line was underscored twice.) The wood's rotten. I'll fix it next time I'm up there.

There's food in the cupboards. Eat it. You're too skinny.

Love,
Petey.

Smiling fondly, Sam tucked the note back into her pocket. The drive from the city had taken most of the day, and the sun was already edging towards the top of the mountains surrounding the lake. Sam hurried back to her car and began bringing in the rest of her luggage.

An easel, watercolours, oils and acrylics, a large wooden box full of mediums, charcoal and pencils, copious brushes, sketchbooks, and a dozen canvasses had filled the boot and both back seats of the car. Sam brought them inside with significantly more care than she'd shown her travel bag, which held only clothes and towels. She placed most of her equipment on the table then opened the easel in the empty space in the room's corner.

Sam adjusted the angle of the easel so that it caught the natural light from the window, and set a canvas on it. It looked good there, she thought. *Like an artist's dream retreat. If this doesn't get you back into your groove, nothing will.*

The sky was darkening quickly, and Sam knelt in front of the fireplace. She found matches and clumsily lit the kindling in the grate. She hadn't started a fire since her parents had taken her camping when she was a child. She used up most of the kindling before the blaze was strong enough to catch onto the larger pieces of wood.

Satisfied that her fire wasn't about to die, Sam went to explore the second floor. The steep, narrow staircase turned at the corner of the room and led straight into a bedroom, which, like the ground floor, was open-plan. There was something resembling a bathroom at the back wall, with a sink, cupboard, mirror, toilet, and a bathtub—but no shower. The sink and bathtub had plugs, but no taps. On examination, Sam found a pipe coming out of the wall, with a drain and a bucket underneath it, set next to a hand pump. She guessed it was connected to a rainwater tank behind the cabin.

Of course. No electricity and no running water.

That meant she would have to heat the water over the fire if she wanted a warm bath. It wouldn't have bothered Peter. He was a mountain man through and through; he loved hunting, fishing, and woodworking, and he probably relished icy-cold showers, too.

A large double bed took up most of the room. It held several layers of thick quilts, topped with animal furs. Sam hesitated, felt the furs gingerly, then folded them up and placed them in the cupboard opposite the bed. Sleeping under the skins of dead animals seemed strangely macabre.

The door leading to the balcony stood to her left. Sam opened it and leaned on the sill to absorb the view. The sun had set behind the mountains, but most of the sky was still a pale blue, with tinges of red showing just above the tops of the trees on the west mountain. The glassy lake, which seemed to stretch on forever, reflected the patchy white clouds. Peter's cabin was set at one of the lake's widest points, but to her right, it narrowed and curved around the sides of the hills that cradled it.

The dock protruded from the shore below the cabin, running twenty meters into the lake. Something large and misshapen sat at its end; Sam squinted in the poor light, trying to make out what it was, then her heart faltered as the shape moved.

It was a man, on his knees, bent over the edge of the dock. His broad shoulders trembled as he stared, fixated on the water below.

CHAPTER 2

Sam's mouth had dried. She squeezed the balcony's bannisters so tightly that her knuckles turned white. Her mind, shocked and panicky, struggled to pull information together. *Who is he?* Peter had said there weren't any other houses within walking distance. *Is he a hiker? Why's he on our dock?*

She was suddenly acutely aware of just how remote the cabin was. If she went missing, no one would know until she failed to return home a week later. The police would take hours to reach her, even if she could call them, which she couldn't. Any defence would have to come from her own hands.

The man wasn't moving, except for his shoulders, which twitched sporadically. Sam backed away from the balcony, barely daring to breathe, keeping her eyes fixed on the man until he disappeared from sight, then she turned and ran down the cabin's stairs.

I need a weapon—something to intimidate him with or use in self-defence. Sam wrenched open the kitchen drawers, searching for a knife, but she came up with only two small blades that were useless for anything more than chopping carrots. She turned to look about the room, bouncing with anxious energy, and a glint of silver beside the fireplace caught her eye. *The axe. Yes, that'll do nicely.*

Sam gripped its wooden handle and raised it to head height. She gave it an experimental swing and staggered as its weight threw her off-balance. Anxious sweat built over her back and palms as she turned towards the door and licked her lips.

He's probably just a hiker who's gone off the path to have a closer look at the lake.

He was trespassing, though, on what was clearly private property. Worse, he had to know someone was staying there—the car parked out front and the fireplace's glow leaking through the windows were impossible to ignore.

The doorknob felt unusually cold under Sam's

fingers. She took a breath to brace herself then shoved the door open and staggered outside, her shaking hands squeezing the axe's handle so tightly that they ached.

Be strong. Be intimidating. Show him that he doesn't want to mess with you.

"Hey, punk, this is private property," she yelled, hoping he wouldn't hear the frightened squeak in her voice. No answer came. Sam squinted at the dock, which was becoming increasingly hard to see in the rapidly failing light. It was empty.

Sam swivelled to look down the length of the shore then turned towards the straggly edges of the forest. The thick shadows created a kaleidoscope of light and darkness. She couldn't see him, but that didn't mean he was gone.

"Did you hear me?" she called, louder this time. "I have a gun and a career in karate."

Complete hyperbole, of course. As a child, she'd had all of two karate lessons before she dropped it in favour of painting classes. The intruder didn't need to know that, though.

Sam listened hard, straining to hear the telltale crunch of footsteps on dry leaves, but, though the woods hummed with the sounds of birds settling down for the night, she couldn't hear any man-made noises. She turned in a complete circle before letting the axe drop to her side, then she returned to the safety of the cabin.

That should have been enough to scare him off, anyway.

Sam took one last look at the lakeshore and the dock then closed the door with a quiet click. The fire had grown nicely, but it had consumed most of the wood, so she dropped the axe back against the wall and knelt to shove fresh logs onto the crackling flames.

The appearance of a stranger in the one place that was supposed to guarantee solitude had shaken her. For all she knew, he could be the only other human for kilometres, and she had no idea who he was or why he'd specifically come to her cabin—or, for that matter, what fascinated him so much about the water at the end of the dock.

Sam rubbed her hands across her face and stood. Worrying wouldn't help her; the man was probably embarrassed at being seen and was already halfway back to his trail. She wouldn't let the fright ruin her first night at the cabin.

As Peter had promised, the kitchen held a large collection of tinned foods. Sam sorted through them, wrinkling her nose at the twelve cases of Spam before picking out a tin of chicken soup. She found a set of pans hanging beside the sink, and spoons in one of the drawers. Unable to find a can opener, Sam eventually resorted to using one of the small knives to cut a hole in the top of the tin to shake the soup through.

She settled back in front of the fire, using thick oven mitts to shield her hands as she held the pot over the flames. Night had well and truly fallen, and the birds were finally silent, giving way to the bats, owls, and other animals of the night. Their calls, alien and jarring, echoed through the woods behind the cabin. The fire was her only source of light, and when the soup was warm enough, she snuggled into one of the armchairs to watch the mesmerising flames while she ate.

The quiet crackle and pop of the fire, the warm soup, and the plush chair conspired to lull her into a comfortable daze, and she didn't even realise she was falling asleep until the spoon fell out of her hand and hit the floor with a loud ping.

"Jeeze, Sam, wake up," she mumbled to herself, and stretched out of the chair. She took the pot and spoon to the sink and, after a moment's confusion, figured out how to get a burst of water from the hand pump. She rinsed her utensils, set them to drain, threw the empty tin into a large garbage bag, then turned to the canvas in the corner of the room.

Tiredness weighed at her limbs, but the week was supposed to be a chance for her to focus on her art, and she wanted to start it on the right foot. The canvas, one of the larger ones in her collection, seemed horribly imposing. She squinted at it, stupidly hopeful that inspiration would appear before her eyes, but all she could think about was how close the exhibition's deadline was and how pulling out a week before the showing would kill her career before it even started.

The more she thought about the deadline, the harder it was to come up with ideas. She turned away from the canvas, blocking the intimidatingly empty rectangle from her sight, and riffled through the cluttered table until she found her sketchbook.

It had been eight months since she'd last drawn in it, and flipping through the pages was like reliving half-forgotten dreams. There were pages full of hand practice—where she'd agonised over getting the knuckles, fingernails, and veins *just right*—then the page full of water textures and lily pads, followed with a pencil drawing of a curious lizard who'd sat outside her window.

She recognised the point where she'd received the invitation to show her work in the prestigious Heritage Gallery: the pages were suddenly saturated with colours, and the pencil lines became a little too wild to convey their shapes properly. Then there were pages and pages of ideas for her showing. Sam flipped to the last page she'd drawn in, which was full of eyes. That was what she'd almost chosen for her gallery: an array of oils featuring eyes gazing out of teacups, eyes blended into nature, eyes appearing in the cracks of sandstone chimneys…

There was one incredibly familiar pair of eyes: her mother's. Sam had drawn them when they'd spent the afternoon at a little café, talking about the show, the possibilities it would open up, and what it meant for Sam's career. And she hadn't even once thought to ask why her mother looked so thin.

Sam slammed the book closed as a bitter taste filled her mouth. The fire was growing low in the grate. If she wanted to stay awake any longer, she would have to add more wood.

No. I'd better to go to bed. I'm probably just worn out from the drive and the stress. I'll start working tomorrow, when I have a clear head.

Sam threw a final regretful look at the empty canvas then returned the sketchbook to the table before climbing the stairs to the bedroom. Heat from the fire had risen to take the worst of the chill out of the upstairs room, but Sam still brushed her teeth feverishly quickly before wriggling under the multiple quilts, fully clothed.

She could see the stars through a gap in the curtains. They were so much brighter than in the city and clustered so thickly that it was almost impossible for her to think she was looking at the same sky as the one she could see from her apartment window. As she closed her eyes and felt the sluggishness of sleep grow over her, her mind returned to the man she'd seen on the dock and the way his shoulders had quivered as he gazed into the water.

CHAPTER 3

Thunk.

Sam jolted awake. Her mind was still half-full of scattered dreams, and she couldn't immediately remember where she was. Pale light streamed through the balcony's glass door, painting colour across the wooden floor, and Sam struggled to get out from under Peter's layered quilts.

What was that noise? It wasn't part of my dream.

The icy early morning air assaulted her feet as soon as soon as she swung them over the edge of the bed.

Sam gasped and pulled on her sneakers with quick tugs. She wished she had a jacket, but all of her clothes were still in the suitcase on the ground floor.

Then the events from the previous day flooded back to her, dispelling the sleepy haze, and Sam lurched to her feet. Her skin prickled as she turned towards the stairwell.

The noise had come from the ground floor. Sam edged towards the stairs and tried to remember if she'd locked the cabin's door. She didn't think so. Her mind immediately went to the man on the dock. *There's no way that guy hung around overnight.*

And yet, *something* had broken through her sleep. It hadn't been a quiet noise, either; it wasn't something that could be explained by the house's wood flexing in the cool or the early morning chatter of birds. Sam wished she'd had the fore-thought to bring the axe upstairs.

She crept down the steps, keeping her breathing and footfalls quiet. When she reached the bend at the corner of the house, she ducked her head to get a look into the lower room. It was empty.

Thank goodness.

That was one good thing about the open-plan building: it left nowhere to hide. Light came through the four windows, scattering shadows under the table and in the corners of the kitchenette. Still, Sam remained alert as she descended the stairs and stood, shivering, in the centre of the room.

If I'm alone, what caused the noise?

The answer came when she glanced towards the cold fireplace. A log had fallen off the wood pile and lay on the fur rug.

Sam let her breathe out in a whoosh and hurried to her travel case. She unzipped it and dug through the clothes to find her thickest jacket and a pair of hiking boots, which she swapped for her thin sneakers. It wasn't enough to stop her from shivering, so she turned towards the fireplace with the intention of lighting it.

She made it halfway across the room before she stopped. She'd been so intent on looking for a stranger in her cabin that two very important changes had escaped her notice. Firstly, there were three mugs laid out on the kitchen bench, just in front of the window overlooking the shrubs behind the cabin. She hadn't used any mugs the day before. The cups had been arranged with precision, too; their handles all pointed in the same direction—towards the easel.

There she found the second change, and it froze her breath in her lungs. Someone had painted on the canvas.

A man's face stared at her from the cloth. It was a closely cropped portrait, realistic and barely dry. Deep-set grey eyes gazed out from above a crooked nose and thin lips. He had thick salt-and-pepper hair and uneven stubble. A red mark—a cut that had not quite healed—marred his cheek.

"Oh," Sam whispered, unable to think of anything else to say. "*Oh.*"

She recognised the style. The thin strokes, the mingling of the colours, and the particular way the hair had been painted were all very familiar, because she'd seen them hundreds of times before.

Either I painted this picture or someone spent an awful lot of time and effort imitating me.

Sam struggled to slow her frantic breathing as her mind snatched at shreds of logic amongst the rising panic. *Am I sure I'm alone?*

The axe was leaning against the wall beside the fireplace, where she'd left it. Sam picked it up and raised it in front of her body, even though it was a struggle to keep it steady. She could think of only a couple of places an average-sized person could hide, and she moved through them quickly. First, she tried the kitchen pantry, which was still stacked with canned soups, pastas, and far too many tins of Spam. Next, she tried the cupboard below the stairs, where she found nothing except a stack of spare blankets and empty buckets.

Sam ran back up the stairs, staggering under the weight of the axe, and into the bedroom. She doubted anyone could have gotten up there without her noticing, but she still checked under the bed and in the wardrobe. Finally, she moved to the balcony and pulled back the thick curtains, exposing a breathtaking view of the outside world.

Mist had rolled in overnight. It covered the ground like a blanket and drifted across the lake in lazy swirls. Sam followed the low-lying clouds to where they rose against the bases of the mountain, clinging to the greenery like a ghostly spiderweb. It was one of the most eerily beautiful things she'd ever seen.

Sam exhaled, and the plume of her breath rose past her to dissolve in the icy air. It had to be early morning; there was enough light to see her way, but the sun hadn't yet topped the mountains in the distance.

Dark motion in the mist caught Sam's attention, and she turned back to the lake. When she squinted through the thick fog, she caught glimpses of... *What? The dock? No... something* on *the dock*.

Sam gasped as another billow of mist engulfed the dark shape. She didn't waste time waiting for the fog to clear, but turned, crossed the room, and took the stairs two at a time. She skidded on the main room's polished wooden floor and hit the door with a thud. Her fingers shook as she fumbled to turn the handle, then she burst through the opening, axe held high, and took two stumbling steps towards the dock.

The mist rolled around her, seeming to pull her into its folds. It was much thicker than it had looked from the upstairs room. It prickled at her cheeks and nose, freezing her lungs when she inhaled. Stepping outside was like entering another dimension; even the sounds from the forest seemed muffled. Sam squinted, searching for shapes amongst the sea of white as she staggered forward.

The beginning of the dock appeared first, the tar-black pillars materialising through the mist like phantom ships. Sam continued until she was even with them then put one hand on the closest pillar. The condensation that had gathered on it trickled down her wrist.

"Hello?" Sam called, but the fog seemed to swallow her voice. She shuddered and glanced at her feet, where the dark planks grew out of the grassy shore. *Peter said not to go on the dock…*

The mist thinned as a gust of wind tore through it, and Sam glimpsed the end of the dock. *Empty.* The black pillars marking the walkway's end were barely visible; beyond them, everything was white. *Is that what I saw? I suppose, in the fog and from a distance, it would be possible to mistake a post for a kneeling person.*

Even so, Sam didn't turn away immediately, but watched as the mist enveloped the dock once again. She felt, deep in her bones, that she wasn't alone. It was one of the most uncanny sensations she'd ever experienced. She let the axe drop and rested its head on the ground, keeping her fingers on the handle to stop it from tipping. Somewhere in the distance, a bird screeched, and a flurry of wings followed as it and its companions took flight. Sam turned, but the mist was too thick to see them.

It was too thick to see *anything*.

Sam tightened her shaking fingers on the axe. She kept turning, searching for a landmark, any shape at all, but all she could see was a wall of white. No trees. No cabin. *It's like I've been transported to another planet.*

The thought frightened her, and she started forward, guessing the direction of the cabin as well as she could. The axe's head dragged over the frosty, sparse grass, and for a moment, the grating noise was all she could hear. Then more birdcalls and whirring wings filled the air, and a tall, familiar outline emerged from the fog.

Thank goodness.

Sam increased her pace to a sprint and pushed through the cabin's door. It was dark inside—darker than she remembered it—but it felt *safe*, and with a sigh, she dropped the axe beside the fireplace.

There wasn't much kindling left, but she managed to light it and spent twenty minutes carefully feeding in the smallest pieces of wood until the fire was strong enough to survive without her. The sun had topped the ridge by the time she looked out the window, and she was surprised to see the fog had almost entirely disappeared. Pockets of it lingered in the corners of the mountainside, and thin wisps were rapidly dissolving from above the smooth surface of the lake.

The dock was easy to see. Its dark wood contrasted with the crisp blue, and the view looked good enough to make a decent painting.

On the subject of paintings…

Sam reluctantly turned to face the portrait in the corner of the room and met the cool-grey eyes of the strangely familiar face.

CHAPTER 4

Sam stepped towards the painting. The eyes transfixed her. The cruel gaze held secrets she never wanted to hear.

She couldn't remember where she knew him from. He definitely wasn't someone she was on first-name basis with. It was a brief familiarity—like someone she'd passed in the street, whose face had been unique enough for her to subconsciously make a note of.

Her apartment was on the outskirts of the state's

largest city. Sam guessed she would have passed at least a hundred new faces each day—and yet, she knew if she'd seen that face before, she wouldn't have forgotten it so easily. *Where'd it come from, then? A dream?*

Yes, she realised. *I did dream him. But not in that way.*

Images rose in her mind when she closed her eyes. She saw herself walking down the stairs and passing the fire, which had been reduced to coals. She'd taken her place in front of the easel, palette in one hand and brush in the other, and painted as though she were in a trance.

Sam pressed her palms to her forehead and rocked on her feet. *I've been sleep-waking, then. Or, rather, sleep-painting…*

She thought she remembered putting the paint in the desk's drawer before returning upstairs. Sure enough, when she opened the drawer, a plastic pallet sat inside, covered with well-blended colours.

It's the stress. I'm panicking about the Heritage show and stranger in the mist, and my brain's blending the ideas and processing them the best way it can.

Sam glanced at the painting again. If it was a message from her subconscious, it didn't bode well: the haggard face, the cruel, hungry expression, and the way the deep grey eyes seemed to follow her… Sam closed the distance between herself and the painting, pulled it off the easel, and propped it against the wall so it faced the wooden planks.

The room was warming up, thanks to the fire, and Sam took off her thick coat and draped it over the back of the chair. She was ravenous. The pantry held a stack of baked bean tins hidden behind the Spam, and she tipped one of them into a blackened pan to heat over the fire.

Sam ate straight out of the pot while she warmed her dew-dampened shoes in front of the fire. By the time she'd finished eating and had washed up, the forest was alive with noises. She checked her phone; it was just after ten in the morning. *Good. Still early enough to have a productive day.*

There weren't any service bars on her mobile, but that was to be expected. She'd been watching the signal on the drive up, and it had disappeared not long before she'd entered the woods. For the rest of the trip, her phone would be a very expensive, cumbersome clock.

Sam stretched, working the tension out of her back and shoulders, then pulled the wooden dining chair up to the easel. She picked out a small canvas, one only a little larger than her head, and set it in place. *A smaller canvas means less space to fill... and less pressure to make it perfect.*

She pulled the pallet out of the drawer and stared at the myriad of blended oil colours. She still found it hard to believe that she'd painted such a coherent image while asleep. Sam pushed the thought from her mind and dabbed her brush into the paint. It was tacky from being left in the drawer overnight, but not completely set, so she grabbed the bottle of primer and added a dollop to loosen the paint. It was an expensive brand of oils, and she didn't want to waste any more than she already had.

A large smudge of green-grey covered one corner of the pallet, so Sam swirled her brush through it and raised her hand to apply it to the canvas. *Okay, Sammy, what are we painting today?*

She hesitated, the brush held a millimetre from the cloth. She hadn't planned anything, and the usual ideas seemed reluctant to enter her mind. All she could think about were the sallow face and cold grey eyes.

Focus! Pick something and put it on the canvas. It's that simple. What about a bird? You used to love painting birds.

Sam lowered the brush and looked at the rest of the colours on the pallet. Dusky pink—that had been for the man's face. The grey-blue had been his flannel top. The dull green, which was currently on her brush, had been used for the trees behind him. And the deep grey, just a tiny amount, was for his irises.

Why can't I get him out of my mind?

"C'mon, Sam," she coached herself, rolling her head to relax the muscles in her neck. "Push through the block. Start freestyle. Paint abstract, even. Just get some colours on the canvas, and it'll get easier—you'll see."

Twenty minutes later, Sam carried the canvas, half-covered in haphazard smears of greens and blues, to the fireplace. She threw it onto the flames and wiped the tear tracks off her cheeks as she watched the wet paint send up plumes of black smoke. The aborted painting took far longer to burn than she was comfortable with.

"Damn it," she hissed, pressing her palms against her eyes to hold back the dampness. "Get it together, Sam. You've only got a week."

She personally knew at least three artists who would have committed first-degree murder for the chance to show their work at the Heritage Gallery. It was the sort of thing an artist put on a resume to raise eyebrows, and the gallery had launched more careers than she could count.

Denzel, her childhood friend, was interning at the Heritage. He'd called in every favour he was owed and blended them with a lot of grovelling and carefully placed hints to work the impossible: a show for Sam, a nearly unheard-of artist.

The gallery's co-ordinator had given Sam eight months to prepare a collection of a dozen exhibits. Eight months had seemed like an eternity at the time, but there she was, with nine days until the matinee night, and nothing was ready. Nothing started.

Nothing even *conceived*.

During the first week following her invite, Sam had felt as though she might explode from all of the possibilities filling her mind. She'd shared them with her mother that crisp autumn morning as they'd enjoyed their coffees at the local café. While they talked, Sam had idly sketched her companion's eyes without fully realising how much they'd sunken in a few short weeks, how gaunt her mother's cheeks were, or how her skin seemed almost papery in the fluorescent light.

Sometimes, Sam wondered if her mother had ever intended to tell her. If she'd known, Sam could have taken time away from her job, moved back in with her mother, and spent as much of those last few days with her only remaining parent as possible. Instead, she'd had to hear it from her mother's doctor at the stroke of midnight. *"The cancer's progressed far more rapidly than we anticipated. If you would like to say goodbye, you'll need to come quickly."*

After that, she'd had only five hours with her mother—to sit beside the hospital bed, stroking the fragile, bone-thin hand resting on starchy white sheets—before the best person in her life had exhaled for the last time.

The following weeks passed like a dream. Sam had struggled to keep the days straight, often missing her shifts at work or turning up on the wrong days. She'd stopped painting—and stopped *thinking* about painting—and the Heritage Gallery invite had been lost at the bottom of a drawer.

She'd emerged from the fog of raw grief as a different person. She still loved painting. That was built into her identity. Nothing on heaven or earth could abolish the joy a loaded brush gave her. But the desire was gone. She was like a starving man whose hunger had been sated; he could gaze at a lavish feast, appreciate its appeal, then shrug and turn away.

Then one day, she'd realised the exhibition was less than two months away, and she hadn't touched a paintbrush in half a year. Panic set in. She'd bought new canvasses, new paints, and a clean set of brushes then tried to create again. The results had disgusted her. *You're just rusty,* she'd told herself as she glared at a horribly proportioned, terribly boring tree she'd created. *Practice will bring it all back.*

Except, it hadn't. She'd tried to start the show's collection a dozen times during those two months and had trashed it every time.

Two weeks out from the exhibition, when Sam had been on the verge of calling Denzel to tearfully, humiliatingly cancel, Uncle Peter had called up like her guardian angel and offered her a week at his cabin. It provided the perfect setting to get her back into her art: there was no contact with the outside world. No distractions. Nothing to do except paint.

But all I have so far is a sleep-created, nightmare-induced face. I can't even imagine what the critics would say if I tried to show that at the Heritage.

Sam watched the fire until it had reduced the canvas to a sad slop on top of the smouldering logs, then she inhaled and leaned back against the armchair. *The week's still young. Twelve paintings is a stretch, but not impossible.*

The cabin smelt awful thanks to the burning chemicals, and the stench churned her stomach. Sam glanced at the window and caught a glimpse of rich green trees and blue skies. The day was too beautiful to spend indoors. *Maybe a taste of nature will give me the kick I need.*

The idea energised her, and Sam pulled on a thin jacket and packed her sketchbook and a box of charcoal pencils into her satchel. She added a water bottle then left the cabin, locking the door on the way out.

The lake's shore looked worlds away from the ethereal visage she'd walked through that morning. Straggly brown-green grass grew in patches amongst the sand that led into the still water. Sam turned right and followed the curving shore around the lake.

About a kilometre along, the steep mountain to her right softened into a slope. Sam made out an overgrown trail leading into the trees, and picked up her pace as she entered it. The trees and vines grew high over her, blocking out almost all of the sunlight, but not even the shade could spare her as the day warmed and the uphill climb made her uncomfortably hot. She stripped off her jacket and tied it around her waist.

The brush became increasingly thick and snaggly as she moved higher. Vines caught at her clothes and twisted across the dirt path, threatening to trip her. She had to stop several times to remove leeches from her legs.

Then the path turned, and Sam found herself facing an open, rocky area. It looked as though a landslide had occurred there a few years back, and it had cleared a gap in the vegetation. Sam climbed one of the higher rocks and settled down to rest on its flat top.

The forest spread out like a green carpet ahead of her, rushing to meet the blue water. She'd travelled farther than she'd expected, and Sam couldn't stop a grin from growing over her face as she spotted her cabin, laughably small, at the edge of the lake.

She closed her eyes and drank in the sensations. The cold rock beneath her was refreshing. Dead and dried leaves under her feet crackled whenever she shifted. Birds screamed in the distance, and insects hummed in the foliage.

Sam pulled the art book out of her satchel. The Heritage's show would need proper canvas paintings, but at least she could sketch some ideas to use as references. She swivelled her wrist to loosen it, then started to draw anything in sight: trees, rocks, leaves, and even her own boots.

A brightly coloured bird flitted out of the bushes and hopped across the rocks. Sam kept her hand moving, but held her breath as she watched the bird. It either hadn't seen her or didn't mind the company as it foraged for insects among the fallen leaves. Then something startled it—Sam couldn't tell if she was guilty or not—and the bird dashed away with a shrill cry.

Sam sighed and glanced at her art book. Shock hit her like a cold slap. In the centre of the paper, surrounded by scribbled plants and indistinct shapes, was a drawing of the man.

CHAPTER 5

Sam couldn't believe what she was seeing. The pencil fell from her grip and hit the forest floor with a dull *tk*, but she barely noticed. The face was looser and messier, but clearly recognisable.

I can't believe I drew that.

Sam closed the art book with a snap, simultaneously creeped out and ashamed. She didn't want to dwell on the image, where she knew the face from, or why her subconscious was bringing it up all of a sudden. The calm, happy mood she'd developed during the hike had dissipated as thoroughly as if someone had thrown water over her.

She packed up her equipment and turned back to the trail. Going left would lead her downhill, towards the cabin, but the path also continued to her right, weaving into the thickening forest. Sam hesitated then turned right. *Now that I'm here, I may as well see where it leads.*

The path took her up the steep incline, zig-zagging through the trees so erratically that Sam started to regret her decision to follow it. Just when she was about to give it up as a futile exercise, the path opened onto a proper hiking trail.

Sam stopped in the middle of the cleared area and took a deep breath, glad to be out of the claustrophobically tight vegetation. She couldn't see any nearby signs, so she turned right and followed the new trail across the length of the mountain.

Occasionally, the path opened onto a lookout with a view of the lake. The cabin was no longer visible, but Sam caught glimpses of hillsides that the curve of the mountains had previously hidden. She followed the trail for a little more than twenty minutes before encountering a blockade. A chain crossed the path, tethered at each end to a metal pole. A placard—facing away from her—hung from its centre.

Sam climbed over the chain to read the sign and frowned.

Trail Closed—Unsafe

The path she'd followed had been wide and well-maintained. *What's unsafe about it?*

A little way ahead of her, the dirt road melted into a clearing. Several other trails split off from it, and a large sign displaying a map stood in the clearing's centre. Sam approached the map and let her eyes rove over the maze of trails circling the lake and surrounding mountains before she spotted a little red marker reading You Are Here.

She traced the paths leading out from her location and found only one that went near Uncle Peter's cabin: the closed one.

Well, at least that means I'll have some privacy.

She thought of the man kneeling on the dock, and shivers crawled down her spine. It was too late to visit any of the other trails, so she turned back to the chained-off path. She had one leg over the barricade when a voice made her jump.

"Ma'am, I'm going to have to ask you to stop."

Sam nearly tripped over the chain, but managed to right herself in time to see the uniformed ranger jogging out of one of the side paths.

"That's a restricted area."

Colour rose across Sam's face. "Sorry—I know—I'm, uh…"

He came to a stop in front of her, breathing deeply but not quite panting. His ranger's uniform, dark green with gold highlights, was well-pressed and clean. Sam felt as though she were being scrutinised, but it was hard to tell thanks to the dark sunglasses he wore under his cap.

"Where're you coming from, ma'am?" His voice was clipped, but not accusatory, and Sam managed to form a coherent answer through her embarrassment and shock. "Sorry—I came from that path. I didn't know it was restricted. I'm staying in the cabin by the lake."

The ranger cocked his head to one side. "Not Peter Mahoney's place?"

"That's it, yeah. I'm his niece."

"Well then." A grin grew across the ranger's sharp jaw, and he took off his glasses. He had bright-blue eyes, which sparkled with faint amusement. "I suppose an apology is in order. I know Pete. He's a good guy. He helped out during the burn-offs last year. I didn't know the cabin was occupied, that's all."

"I'm only staying a week." Sam glanced at the trail behind her. "Is it okay for me to go back that way?"

"Sure thing. Just be careful. There've been some

accidents along that path lately. Don't stray into the forest, and watch out for falling rocks, okay?"

Sam nodded. She couldn't imagine how the flat, orderly trail could be any more dangerous than the others criss-crossing the mountains—but then, maybe the problem section came farther along, past where she turned off into the smaller path leading to the cabin.

An idea struck her, and she glanced back at the ranger. "Uh, if you don't mind me asking—"

"Go right ahead, ma'am." He'd relaxed and was watching her with evident amusement.

Sam wondered if she looked as sweaty and dishevelled as she felt. She tried to stand a little taller, hoping he wouldn't notice her embarrassed flush. "Are there any properties on the lake? Other than Peter's, I mean."

His eyebrows rose. "Now that's an odd question. Not as far as I know. From what I heard, Peter was friendly with a couple of the councilmen, which is how he got permission to build there. Otherwise, the whole area is government owned. But then, I'm only in charge of the northern region of the forest. The lake itself is a state issue."

"Right." Sam turned towards the path, but the ranger stopped her.

"Why the question, ma'am?"

She hesitated, wondering how much to tell him.

"It's just—a man was hanging around the dock in front of the property last night. I wasn't sure if he lived in the area or was a hiker, but, uh…" She trailed off and waved a hand towards the chain's sign.

The ranger's face was unreadable, but the business-like clip had returned to his voice. "Well, I can't discount that someone climbed over the chain. I try to keep an eye on it, but there's only so much time I can spend around this area."

"Right. Of course."

"You haven't seen anyone since then, have you?"

Sam thought of the dark shape barely visible through the swirling fog that morning. "No."

"Hmm." The ranger watched her for a moment, a slight frown hovering over his blue eyes, then he unclipped a black box from his belt. "Better safe than sorry. Take my walkie-talkie; it's the only thing that can be used to communicate around here unless you have a two-way radio. This'll get you direct communication with the ranger's station, though, and there's almost always someone there if you need help."

"Oh!" Sam took the black box and smiled at it. "Hey, thanks."

"No problem. Drop it off at the office when you leave, okay? My boss would kill me if I lost it."

"Sure, I'll do that."

The ranger flashed her another smile as he tipped

his hat. "You have a nice day, ma'am."

He watched her as she climbed over the fence, and didn't turn away until the curve of the path hid her from sight.

CHAPTER 6

The walk up to the clearing had taken three hours. The hike back down seemed to take twice as long. By the time she stepped onto the lakeshore, Sam was exhausted and famished. She felt incredibly stupid for walking so far with only a bottle of water.

The sun was already passing behind the high mountains when she stumbled into the cabin and tugged off her boots. She massaged the blister that had formed on her right foot, then, grumbling to herself, she snatched up the more comfortable sneakers.

The cabin had retained a lot of the heat from the now-dead fire, but she knew the warmth wouldn't last long as night set in. She toyed with the idea of going straight to bed without bothering to rekindle the fire, but she knew she would regret it when she had to get up in the freezing morning. *Besides, I could really go for some hot soup right now.*

That meant she would need kindling. Sam sighed and tied the sneakers, tossed her satchel onto the table, and left the comfort of the cabin. She turned towards the forest, aiming for the closest crop of trees, but a flash of motion in her peripheral vision stopped her. She turned so quickly that she nearly slipped in the gritty sand, but there was nothing to see: just the empty dock and the glassy water.

Sam approached the pier, keeping her senses on high alert. She could have sworn she'd seen something move on it. *The man came back*, her mind insisted. But the dock was empty, and there was nowhere for a person to hide—without jumping into the lake, which was impossible. The water was still.

The sensation of no longer being alone, the same one she'd felt when she'd arrived, washed over her. Sam hesitated at the base of the dock, scanning the shore, the still water, the gently swaying trees, and the clear patch surrounding the cabin.

You're alone, she told herself, trying to convince her frantic, galloping heart. *There's no one for miles.*

An exhale, so faint that she could barely hear it over the drum of her pulse, seemed to rush through her. It sounded raw and raspy, as though the air had been pulled through a damaged throat.

You imagined it. There's nothing. Nothing except the wind in the trees and your stupid imagination going wild—

She could feel eyes on her, watching her, quietly delighted to see while not being seen.

Stop it, stop it, stop it—

Then an owl, tired of waiting for the sun to finish its descent behind the mountains, screeched. Sam jumped. She was shocked to find she'd been holding her breath, and she drew in a lungful of oxygen with a deep shudder. The lake was still. The shore was empty. It was getting dark, and she had a fire to start.

Shaky and a little embarrassed, Sam hurried towards the forest. An abundance of small, dry sticks lay amongst the fallen leaves, and Sam gathered an armful before returning to the cabin. There was still plenty of wood in the bracket beside the fireplace, so Sam locked the cabin's door and settled down for the night as the last of the sunlight disappeared over the ridge.

The soup—two tins of chicken and vegetables heated over the fire—was delicious. Sam sipped at it as she rubbed her aching feet over the plush fireside rug. She wished she'd brought a novel. While packing for the trip, she'd imagined herself consumed with creative inspiration and painting late into the night, but she was starting to realise how unrealistic that was. After her day of hiking, she couldn't tolerate even the idea of trying to work. All she wanted was to lounge in front of the fire and watch a movie or lose herself in a good book.

She'd searched the cupboards in the vague hope that Peter would have brought a book on one of his weekend trips, but all she'd come up with was a technical manual for lacquering techniques, a pack of cards, and the radio he'd mentioned in his letter.

The radio was better than nothing, so Sam filled it with batteries and turned it on. It caught only one station, but she supposed she shouldn't have been surprised. She was so far out from civilisation that she was lucky to have even that. It seemed to be a variety station that ran interviews, programs it had obviously bought from larger stations, songs she'd never heard before, and even the sequelised reading of a novel.

Sam put the empty pot on the floor beside her chair and relaxed into the cushions. She closed her eyes as she listened to the presenter—a man with an old, crackly voice, who called himself Uncle Earnest—read that evening's news.

It was the standard fare: politicians bickering over

a new bill, a natural disaster threatening a country on the other side of the globe, and an update on the Green Energy project. Sam let the words drift over her, feeling strangely detached from the events affecting the rest of the world.

"And now for some local news," Uncle Earnest said. There was a pause as he rustled through his papers.

Sam felt her eyes start to drift closed as she watched the fire spit up sparks.

"For those fine souls in Spring Valley, you'll be happy to know the dam has been successfully repaired, and your homes are once again safe. We've had another report of a giant panther sighting, this time in Clearview. And for any of you good folk living near Harob Lake—"

Sam's eyes snapped open.

"Police have called off the search for Ian McKeller nearly two weeks after his disappearance. He's the fifth this year, so take care if you plan to visit the lake. Up next, we have some local talent, Jamie and the Spitfires, performing a song of their own creation, 'Dreaming of Hills'. Enjoy!"

The country ballad was completely uninspired and sung by a nasally teenager, but Sam barely noticed. She sat completely still, hands clenched on the chair's armrests, staring at the radio. *Fifth this year... does he mean it's the fifth disappearance? Was Ian a tourist, or did he*

live near here? And what part of Harob Lake?
Remembering the chain across the trail, Sam shivered.
She felt in her pockets for her mobile to call Uncle
Peter, then remembered it didn't have any reception.

The cabin felt simultaneously too small and too
large. The fire brightened and warmed the area
immediately in front it, but leaping shadows
dominated the rest of the room. Sam went to the
kitchen, felt in the drawer for the candles she'd seen
there the previous day, and lit five of them, placing
them on plates in strategic locations around the room.
They helped a little, but not enough to keep her from
shivering as she returned to the fire.

The dreadful country song finished, and Uncle
Earnest introduced a segment on financial planning.
Sam threw a fresh log on the fire then coiled in the
chair, wrapping her arms around her torso. The next
news segment would be in an hour; if she was lucky,
Earnest would share more details about Ian McKeller.
In the meantime, she could let the trite talk programs
and country music distract her.

CHAPTER 7

The radio was still playing when Sam woke the next morning. She'd collapsed sideways in the chair, and her neck and back ached from the awkward position. She pulled herself upright with a groan and tried to stretch some of the soreness out.

Light streamed through the cracks in the curtains, splashing long strips of gold across the wooden floor. The fire had reduced to embers, leaving the air brisk, but not as cold as it otherwise would have been.

The radio was playing a morning program that felt a little too chirpy and energetic to match Sam's emotions, so she fumbled with the contraption until she managed to turn it off. Silence rushed in to take its place. Sam sighed and drew a hand through her hair. She felt greasy and gritty, and desperately needed a shower. She'd meant to have one the previous night, before bed, but nothing about that day had gone according to plan.

Then she glanced about the room and did a double-take. A new painting sat on the easel. Sam's stagnant heart rate spiked, and shaking off her grogginess, she crossed the room in three paces.

Once again, her own hand had clearly made the brush strokes. The painting depicted a moonlit forest scene. Sick, strangely shaped trees clustered on either side of an overgrown path. Striding down the path, his grim grey eyes staring out from the paint and an axe clasped in his right hand, was the man.

Sam closed her eyes and rubbed her palms across her temples. The memories were hazy and dream-like, but she recalled approaching the easel, squeezing paint onto the pallet, blending, dabbing, and drawing stripes of colour across the canvas. She'd then left the cups on the bench before returning to the fireside chair.

She turned towards the kitchen. Sure enough, two cups stood in front of the sink, their handles pointing at the easel. *There were three yesterday. Is that significant, or is it just my dream-self getting lazy?*

Sam plucked the painting off the easel, intending to lean it against the wall next to its companion, and froze. A second, smaller painting rested behind the first. The image was set underwater, facing the surface. The dark water was swirling and full of bubbles. It was less detailed than the previous images—more rushed, almost as if she'd been frantic when creating it—but the moon, shining through the frenzy, was unmistakable.

"Jeeze," Sam hissed. Like with the first painting, she turned both of the new ones so that they faced the wall.

What on earth possessed me to create stuff like this? Is it really from stress? Because I've had plenty of stress over the last year, and all it's done is wear down my immune system. Maybe that's the point, though. Maybe this holiday is letting me reacquaint myself with my feelings, and it's like opening a floodgate. These could be repressed emotions spilling onto the canvas. Damn. Wish they'd spill in a more cohesive, marketable way.

Sam found the palette in the drawer and rinsed the half-dried paint down the sink. The water, fresh from the tank behind the cabin, was ice cold. *I'd probably die if I tried to bathe in this.* Sam turned towards the fireplace and scrunched her nose when she saw only two small pieces of wood left in the bracket. *Not enough to heat water* and *cook breakfast.*

Sam pulled on her boots and heavy jacket and pushed open the door. It was later than she'd thought; the sun was already above the mountains. The mist had all but disappeared, though it had left the grass damp. The lake was stunning; its smooth water reflected the fluffy white clouds trailing across the sky and the rich-green mountains. The dock was empty, but the water just beyond it rippled, probably from a fish that had become a little too enthusiastic in the morning light.

Sam jogged the dozen paces between the cabin and the small shed and wrenched open its door. The inside was exactly how she'd imagined it: a haven for a mountain man at heart. A workbench ran along one wall, covered with sanders, grinders, circular saws, and goodness knew what else. A canoe rested on a pallet, taking up most of the right side of the shed. Sam ran her hand across the dark wood appreciatively. *I'd love to take this out on the lake before the week's over.*

The huge stack of firewood waited for her at the back of the shed. A wheelbarrow lay next to it, and Sam hurried to load it up with the logs then pulled it out of the shed. When she turned towards the cabin, the ripples hadn't disappeared from the lake. In fact, they'd intensified.

Water frothed and churned as something struggled

just under the surface. The ripples, which had at first lapped peacefully against the shore, were battering at it, surging forward and retreating like small waves.

Sam stared, her mouth open. She couldn't see what was causing the disturbance, but it had to be big. *What kinds of fish live in this lake?*

The water roiled, spraying droplets high into the air. Dark mud, drawn up from the lake's floor, stained the crystal-blue water black, slowly bleeding out from the frenzy.

Then, as though a switch had been flicked, it stopped. The miniature waves bumped into the dock's pillars and spent themselves on the shore as the lake's surface stilled.

Sam dropped the wheelbarrow and approached the water's edge. The disturbance had been just past the dock. If she stood on the end of the pier, she might be able to see the cause.

Don't go onto the dock. The phrase from Peter's letter echoed in her head as she eyed the wood. It looked solid. But her uncle *had* underlined his warning twice.

Caution won out, and Sam reluctantly returned to her burden. The wood had spilled when she'd dropped the wheelbarrow, and she grumbled as she righted and refilled it.

It only took a few minutes to transfer the logs into the bracket beside the fireplace, then Sam returned the wheelbarrow to the shed. She kept one eye on the water as she passed the lake, but it didn't repeat its antics.

Bathing in the wilderness was a new experience for Sam. She heated pots of water over the fire, carried them upstairs to the bathtub, and mixed in enough cold water from the pump to bring it to a tolerable temperature. She'd forgotten to bring soap, so she used shampoo instead. It wasn't until she'd drained the dirty water that she realised she'd forgotten to boil anything to rinse herself with. She swore under her breath, pumped a few bursts of the icy tank water into the tub, and splashed it over herself as quickly as she could.

She was shivering by the time she drained the bath for the second time and wrapped herself in the two towels she'd brought. Sam hurried downstairs to where the fire crackled pleasantly, and warmed herself while she dried her hair.

It was past lunch by the time she'd finished dressing, and she set to exploring the depths of the pantry. She decided it wasn't a day to be healthy, so she pushed the beans, Spam, and tinned vegetables to one side and eventually settled on a cup of instant noodles.

Sam planned her day while she ate. She had less

than four hours of daylight left. Part of her wanted to pull the canoe out from the shed and take a spin on the lake, but she squashed the idea quickly. Whatever had stirred up the water must have been strong, and there was no guarantee that being in a canoe would keep her safe. Insane ideas rose in the back of her mind—*What if the lake has freshwater sharks or even Harob's own version of the Loch Ness Monster?*—and even though she could laugh at them, she couldn't entirely dismiss them.

The second reason against going onto the lake was the entire purpose of the trip: she had five days left to create twelve paintings. Time wasn't in her favour.

Sam washed up quickly then set a fresh canvas onto the easel. She laid her best set of oils on the table, opened her favourite roll of brushes, and stared at the blank cloth.

Okay, Sam, what are we painting? The grey eyes flashed into her mind, but she pushed them back out. *Nope, not today. How about a corrupted classic? They're a little cheesy, but at least they won't be met with complete derision by the art elite.*

Sam took a soft pencil and sketched the faint outline of a bowl of fruit onto the canvas. She didn't have any references, but she thought it came out reasonably well. She added some maggots crawling out of the apple and dripping onto the crocheted cloth below the bowl, then squeezed the appropriate oil colours onto her palette.

The painting started well. She applied the dark colours first then built up to the light. The bowl was steel grey. *The same grey as his eyes*, she realised, before continuing hurriedly. She used slightly off colours for the fruit. Twenty minutes later, she stepped back from the painting and felt distaste scrunch her lips. The perspective was weird, and she wasn't sure how to fix it. Sam gritted her teeth and switched to painting the background, which was normally the easiest part for her. The lines kept coming out crooked, though, no matter how often she painted over them.

"Damn it," she hissed, dropping the brush back onto the palette. "Get a grip."

It's the water. I can't get it out of my head. The way it churned and dug up mud… I've got to know what's in there.

"Fine," she said, letting her frustration bleed into decisive action. "Fine. We'll take a look at the creepy lake then. We'll prove there's nothing to be frightened of, and when we come back, we'll be able to focus on our work. Okay? Okay."

CHAPTER 8

The lake was perfectly still when Sam left the cabin. She went to the shed, unlocked it, and began dragging the canoe off its pallet.

It was much heavier than she'd anticipated. She got the boat off its stand without too much effort, but pulling it to the water's edge exhausted her. Sam left it on the shore while she returned to the cabin, changed into her swimsuit, and collected one of the still-damp towels. She retrieved the paddle from the shed, tossed it and the towel inside the canoe, then gave it one final, hard shove into the lake. As soon as it came free from the shore, it started drifting away, and Sam hurried after it, wading waist-deep before catching its edge. The water was cold, and the sandy lake floor felt slimy between her toes. Sam grimaced, imagining the multitude of tiny creatures that were probably flittering around her feet.

She nearly tipped the canoe the first time she tried to pull herself into it, but eventually, she managed to haul herself over its edge and collapsed inside. The vessel rocked wildly, and Sam waited until it had stilled before climbing into the seat, wrapping the towel around her waist and picking up the paddle.

She had never been canoeing before, but it had looked easy enough in the commercials she'd seen on TV. She dipped her paddle into the water and pushed a little too hard. The canoe rocked again as it turned.

"Easy," Sam muttered, switching the paddle to the opposite side and trying to ignore the sensation of cold water dripping down her arms. It took a few minutes for her to figure out a system, but then the boat started moving forward, slowly at first, but picking up speed as she alternated sides every two strokes.

Sam turned her canoe towards the end of the dock and drew as close as she dared. The worst of the sediment had cleared since that morning, but the water was still cloudy. Sam squinted, trying to make out shapes through the haze, but it was impossible.

Whatever it was probably moved on ages ago, anyway.

Sam turned the boat towards the opposite side of the lake and picked up speed. She was starting to love the sway of the canoe, the splashing noises the paddle made each time she drew it through the water, and the way the breeze cut through the sun's heat. The lake was too wide to travel to the opposite end and back before the sun dipped behind the mountains, but Sam reached the halfway point before reluctantly turning around.

The cabin stood out like a dark rock against the grey-green woods. It was the first time Sam had seen the mountains behind her home clearly, and she soaked in the view. She could see a crop of rocks halfway up the hill that she thought might have been where she'd stopped during the previous day's hike. Farther up and to the right was a slight gap in the trees—probably one of the viewing spots from the trail. Not far above her cabin, a craggy ledge jutted out from the mountain.

And on the ledge stood a man.

Sam's mouth opened in a silent gasp. The stranger's pose was stiff, except for his arms, which hung limply at his sides. He was too far away for her to see him clearly, but Sam thought he seemed tall and lean and wore dark clothes.

Calm down. It's just a hiker. So what if he ignored the warning sign and crossed over the chain? I'm sure plenty of people do that. It's not like he's the same man who was on the dock or anything. He wasn't carrying a backpack or equipment, though.

The man turned his head, and Sam followed his gaze. He was looking at the cabin. Sam's heart fluttered, but some primitive instinct told her to keep still.

Then the man looked back at the lake, and Sam felt their eyes meet. *I'll bet they're grey*, she thought as her stomach turned cold.

The man held the gaze for half a minute then turned and disappeared into the forest.

Sam sucked in a deep breath. Panic, hot and irrational, coursed through her. She began paddling as a sense of urgency overwhelmed her. *How long would it take him to reach the cabin? Could he get there first if he ran?*

Her arms ached as seldom-used muscles were taxed, but Sam pushed herself to move the canoe as fast as she was capable, single-mindedly focussed on getting to the safety of the cabin and the reassuringly heavy axe.

The familiar hum of insects filled her ears as she drew closer to the shore. Sam's eyes were scanning the mountain, searching for movement between the trees, and she didn't notice immediately when her paddle snagged in a patch of weeds. The plants nearly tugged the paddle out of her hands, but she twisted in her seat and managed to keep her grip. That turned out to be a mistake. The force of the abrupt stop, combined with the way she'd turned her body, tipped the canoe and plunged her into the water.

The lake was ice cold. Sam thrashed, trying to right herself. Her limbs brushed through the dense weeds, and their slimy leaves made her gasp as they swept over exposed skin. Water rushed into her mouth, but she bit down on it before it could fill her lungs. Her feet couldn't find the floor. A flicker of sunlight penetrated the dark water, and Sam struggled towards it, her lungs burning, her heart thundering.

Panic had clouded her mind, and she didn't see the shadowy shape drifting above her. Instead of breaking through the surface, her head rushed up to meet the canoe's hull. Sparks of light shot across her vision, and water filled her lungs as she cried out. Her limbs felt heavier than rocks; she tried to move them, but they only weighted her down, pulling her deeper into the lake. The canoe drifted in front of the sparkling sunlight, leaving her smothered in the weed-choked, muddy shadows.

Hands crept out from between the dense water plants. Ghost white and bone thin, they caressed her skin, tangled in her hair, and tugged at her ankles. There were dozens of them. Sam had a vague idea that they should have bothered her, but all she cared about was finding the energy to take another breath as the blackness crept across her vision.

CHAPTER 9

Sam woke in the cabin, lying on the rug in front of the dying fire. Her lungs felt sore, and stabbing pains extended from a spot just above her temple. She tried to sit up but thought better of it as her stomach threatened to empty itself.

How'd I get here?

Keeping her head as still as possible, Sam let her eyes rove around the room. Everything was quiet. She seemed to be alone.

A new painting stood on the easel. Someone—

I?—had painted over the malformed fruit still life. The steel grey bowl had been turned into a large rock, and the draping background fabric had become trees, while the tabletop had been altered into bushy vegetation.

In place of the rotting fruit stood a man. It was a familiar image. She'd seen it earlier that day, albeit from a distance. Although she hadn't been able to see the man clearly from her canoe, she'd painted him the familiar, haggard, sallow face that had been haunting her.

As soon as she thought she had control over her body, Sam staggered to her feet. She was dizzy, but all of her limbs seemed to work. She hobbled to the door and tried the handle—it had been locked from the inside. She unbolted the latch, opened the door a crack, and looked outside. The canoe rested on the shore, with one end barely touching the smooth water. She couldn't see any other signs of interference.

Sam closed and re-locked the door. The axe still stood beside the fireplace, but unwilling to trust herself with it, she picked one of the paring knives out of the kitchen drawer instead. The blade was far too small to look even remotely threatening, but Sam still held it ahead of herself as she clambered up the stairs.

It only took a minute to search the bedroom and

assure herself that she was definitely alone. She returned downstairs, tossed the knife towards the kitchen, and slumped into one of the overstuffed lounge chairs. Too physically drained to even cry, she watched the fireplace's glowing embers fade into ash.

She slipped into a tenuous, disjointed dream. She saw herself pulling the canoe out of the river, locking herself in the cabin, and painting as blood dripped down her face. Every time she stirred towards wakefulness, she felt the man in the painting watching her, his cold grey eyes fixed on the back of her head with an animalistic hunger.

It was dark when Sam pulled herself together enough to light the candles and draw a drink from the pump by the sink. She leaned on the bench while she savoured the taste of the cold, clean water and tried to clear her head.

She didn't seem seriously hurt. Her vision wasn't blurry, and the dizziness had passed following her nap, so she doubted she was in imminent danger of brain damage. She let her mind drift to less certain ideas.

A man had been watching her from the rock. The following hours were foggy, but she was certain of that, at least. She'd assumed he was a hiker stopping to admire the view, but she felt less confident of that as she remembered the way he'd glanced towards the cabin, as though he'd known exactly where to look. That, combined with the figure she'd seen on the dock and the nightmarish paintings she'd been creating in her sleep, made her deeply uneasy.

Sam approached the table. Amongst the jumble of paint boxes, pencils, and papers, she found the black walkie-talkie the ranger had given her.

It seemed simple enough; a red button sat on top, next to a dial to adjust the volume. *It's got to be after six. There's probably no one at the office.*

Sam pressed the button and cautiously said, "Hello?"

To her surprise, the speaker crackled when she released the button, and a terse female voice answered, "This is the Harob Park Rangers Office. Who's speaking, please?"

"Oh." Sam had been hoping to get straight through to the ranger she'd met the previous day, and wasn't sure she wanted to explain her concerns to the unexpectedly cold voice. She cleared her throat and pressed the button again. "Hi, my name's Sam. I'm staying in the cabin by the lake. I spoke to a ranger yesterday, and he gave me his walkie-talkie—is he available, please?"

A tsk of irritation came from the speakers. "Would that have been Brandon or Tom?"

"Uhh… I'm not sure, sorry. He didn't tell me his name."

"Probably Brandon," the woman said, more to herself than Sam. "He's already left for the day. Do you need emergency assistance?"

Sam felt unsteady on her feet, so she dropped onto the couch and wet her lips. The woman's voice was cold. *Unfeeling*. Still, hostile help was better than no help, so she said, "I heard on the radio that there have been disappearances around Harob Lake."

"Yes," the woman said after a brief pause. "There have been missing-person cases. They occur in any inhospitable region that's frequented by tourists."

"Were any of them found?"

Another *tsk*. "The forest spans more than eighteen square kilometres, much of it mountainous and unchartered. We make every effort to locate missing persons, but the odds are very much against us."

Sam's mouth was dry. She licked her lips again. "So… no? You didn't find them? Not even their bodies?"

"Look," the woman said, and the walkie-talkie's crackle couldn't mask her irritation. "We maintain the trails and post signs, but there's very little we can do if an inexperienced hiker strays off the paths and becomes lost."

Sam knew her companion's patience was wearing thin, but she couldn't stop herself from saying, "The path going near my cabin was cordoned off. Is it because people have gone missing on it? More than normal, I mean?"

"I'm not at liberty to discuss the details of unresolved cases." The ranger's voice could have frozen hell. "But I can assure you, provided you take proper safety precautions when hiking, you are at no greater risk than in any other remote, densely wooded area. Now, if there's nothing else I can help you with, I would appreciate it if we could keep this line clear in case of actual emergencies."

"Oh, yeah, sure. Sorry." Sam let the walkie-talkie fall silent. She sat for a long time, staring at the empty fireplace, chewing over her options. The woman's refusal to answer was almost as good as an affirmative: the trail had been closed because people had gone missing on it, and they considered it too dangerous to keep open. Not that it had bothered the mysterious hiker.

I could leave, Sam thought as she stared at the three paintings propped against the wall, their ghastly images facing away so that she wouldn't have to see them.

Part of her wanted to go—to get out of the cloistered forest and back to her familiar, over-populated city—but she knew she'd never forgive herself if she did. She'd been so grateful for the week in the cabin; it was a merciful lifeline, a final chance to prepare for the Heritage and save her reputation and budding career. She couldn't throw it away just because a hiker didn't like obeying caution signs.

Still, the missing-person cases bothered her.

Sam stretched to shake some of the soreness out of her shoulders and back. The candles were doing a poor job of lighting the cabin, and cold night air was starting to creep in. Sam was acutely aware of how lonely the night felt, so she turned on the radio while she lit the fire.

Uncle Earnest was back, his scratchy voice introducing his eclectic range of songs and talk shows. Sam was tipping a tin of minestrone soup into a pot when he said, "Don't forget, if you have a tip or a news story you'd like to share with our listeners, you can call us on—"

Damn, wish my phone had reception. I bet he'd be more than happy to share what he knows about the missing hikers.

"Or," Earnest continued, "if you have a two-way radio, you can reach us on the following frequency..."

Sam gasped. She might not have a mobile, but the radio *was* two-way. She shoved her dinner onto the bench and ran to the black box.

CHAPTER 10

Sam managed to connect just as Earnest finished introducing a bizarre disco song. She turned the radio's volume down and held her breath.

"Well, hello!" Earnest said after a moment. He sounded delighted. Sam wondered how often he had callers. "How's tonight treating you, darlin'?"

Could be better. "Fine, thanks. Uh, I've been listening to your show, and yesterday you said something about the police calling off the search—"

"For Ian McKeller? Yes, yes, that's right. Dreadful

tragedy. Are you familiar with him?"

Just as she'd hoped, Earnest was keen to talk. Sam mumbled a vague question, and the radio host happily launched into his story.

"Oh, yes, he's the fifth one this year. *Only* this year, mind. There were another four last year, and the rangers' office won't tell me how many there were the year before. It's a dreadful thing. Often they're inexperienced hikers, see, but not always. Ian, for instance, had been bushwalking for decades. I watched an interview with his family. They say he was very cautious about where he went. I suppose he hadn't heard the rumours about Trail T-1."

"Trail T-1?" Sam prompted.

"That's the trail that loops down the southern side of Harob Lake. It's where almost all of the disappearances have happened. Apparently, the council cordoned it off when Ian didn't return, though it's technically no more dangerous than any other trail over the mountains. The rangers say it's a string of *bad luck*." Earnest snorted to show how little he believed in luck. "Want to know what I think?"

Sam's knuckles were white from gripping the edge of the table. "Yes, please."

"Hold on, the song's finishing. Be back in a moment, darlin'."

Sam gritted her teeth and waited for Earnest to finish introducing a new song. When he came back, his voice was muffled as though he had something in his mouth. *Is he eating his dinner?*

"Right, so we were talking about Trail T1, weren't we? Yeah, well, these missing person cases only started about eighteen years ago. Before then, it had been decades since a soul had gone missing around that part of the lake. Then Michael Paluhik and his friends went off the trail."

There were slurping noises as Earnest drank. Sam wanted to believe it was only soda.

"Michael was one of those intense kids, y'know? From what I can gather, he was bullied as a child, but did okay for himself during his teenage years. He had trouble holding down jobs. Some people say he was fired five times in three years, others say it's three in five, and still others say he wasn't fired, but quit every time. Either way, he ended up unemployed at age twenty-six and organised a backpacking trip with two of his friends. They'd only been at it for two weeks when they decided to take a detour and hike through one of the iconic Harob Forest trails. Can you guess which one?"

"Trail T-1," Sam breathed, the image of the swinging warning sign fluttering through her mind.

"Bingo. Michael and his companions were seen entering the trail, but they never came back out."

"Wait." Sam rubbed at her eyes, which were becoming dry and irritated in the fire's light. "How come you use Michael's name, but not his companions'? What's special about him?"

"Because they never found his body," Earnest said patiently. "His two buddies, Troy and Evan, both turned up after three weeks. Badly decomposed, of course, and mostly eaten away by scavengers and insects. They were found a long way off the trail, but even though searches for Michael continued, his body remains lost. Oh, damn it—I missed the song's end. Hang on. Gotta get the botany interview set up."

Sam found it increasingly hard to be patient as her eccentric host spent two rambling minutes discussing his love for hyacinths before starting the pre-recorded interview. He paused to take another long, loud swig before saying, "Sorry, what were we talking about, again?"

His voice was definitely starting to slur. Sam suspected the drinking was a nightly ritual for him. She wondered how long he normally managed to maintain the show before becoming completely incoherent.

"They never found Michael's body?" she prompted.

"That's right," he said, a little too enthusiastic. "And that started a spate of missing people. And missing bodies. What I mean to say is, the people went missing, and their bodies couldn't be found."

"Right," Sam said, trying, and failing, to follow his

logic. "And you think it's all tied to Michael—"

"It's all *because* of Michael, darlin'! Don't you see? His soul can't rest as long as his body is missing. He's become a, uh, not a regular ghost, but one of the over-charged ghosts. What do you call them? Poltergeists. That's it. He's become a poltergeist."

"Ah." Sam squeezed her lips together as she tried to decide whether she wanted to laugh or groan. "Of course."

"I'm glad you have an open mind," Earnest said, completely missing the disappointed note in Sam's voice. "A lot of people baulk as soon as they hear the word *ghost*. But it explains *everything*. Have you heard the rumours about a mysterious, shadowed figure that stalks through the woods? They're not just rumours. I bumped into one of the rangers at the pub last week. Nice guy, y'know, but he looked pretty shaken up. After a bit of prodding, he told me why. He'd been helping look for Ian McKeller. The search parties were all called off at sundown—it's too dangerous to be stumbling through the woods in the dark, yeah?— but this ranger had stayed on a bit longer. He knew the pathways well enough and had enough hiking experience to keep reasonably safe, so he continued searching until just after night had fallen. He said he was on his way back to the base when he saw a dark figure watching him from between the trees."

Sam frowned at the radio. She wasn't sure what to

make of the story; Uncle Earnest was clearly a good way to being drunk, but he also sounded sincere.

"Well," the radio host continued, completely oblivious that the brief gardening interview had ended and his station was broadcasting silence, "he said it was the shock of his life. He called out to the figure, but it turned around and—these are his own words, mind—melted into the trees. For a moment, he thought it might be Ian, so he followed, but pretty quickly realised it couldn't be the missing hiker. Ian had red hair, y'see, and this stranger's was salt and pepper."

Sam reflexively turned to the painting behind her. The sallow man stared back, his salt-and-pepper hair an unkempt mess.

Then she remembered Brandon, the ranger she'd met on the trail, and the brisk, clipped note that had entered his voice when she'd told him about the stranger on her dock. *Brandon couldn't be the ranger Earnest met in the pub, could he...?*

It made sense. Brandon hadn't told her about the figure he'd seen during the search—of course he couldn't have—because it was just that: an obscure figure. His boss, the brisk lady at the ranger's office, probably would have told him he wasn't supposed to alarm the visitors. But it had worried him enough to give Sam his walkie-talkie. *"Better safe than sorry."*

Sam wet her lips. "And so... uh... you think that

Michael's ghost is hanging around the lake?"

"It's possible it's a ghost," Uncle Earnest said, clearly enjoying having a captivated listener. "But I think it's more likely a poltergeist. They're the stronger type of spirit, y'know? They can move stuff and throw stuff. They could even push you over the edge of a cliff, if they wanted to."

"Ah." Sam finally caught up with her friend's mind. "You think he's killing the hikers."

"Absolutely," Earnest said. "Why else would so many hikers be going missing on the same trail? I'll bet Michael's body's lost in a gully somewhere, and when strangers pass by his resting place, he'll give them a shove or throw rocks at them or something, so that he'll not have to be alone anymore."

It's a ridiculous idea, Sam told herself, clenching her fists in her lap to stop their trembling. *Laughable, really.*

"Welp." Uncle Earnest sounded relaxed and a little sleepy. "I'd say it's about time to wrap up this radio program. Thanks for the chat, darlin'. It's always a pleasure to find someone equally interested in the supernatural. Call me up again another time, and I'll tell you about the giant panther that's currently plaguing Pleasantview."

"Sure thing," Sam said, trying to smile. "Thanks."

"Any time, darlin'."

Sam turned off the radio. The fire had nearly eaten through its wood, so she added two new logs before sitting back in the chair and letting her thoughts consume her.

CHAPTER 11

Sam woke with a jolt. She wasn't in the plush armchair anymore, but was standing in front of the easel. Her left hand held a pallet filled with swirls of well-blended paint, and her right was clasped around a paintbrush that barely touched the canvas.

She took a shaky breath and stepped back from the image. Though well painted, it shocked her deeply. *That came from me,* she realised, glancing at the vivid red paint soaked into her brush. *I created that.*

The man crouched on top of a shadowed, limp figure. His grey eyes, which were turned towards the painter, shone in the same way a wolf's did when it savoured the blood of a freshly felled victim… which was exactly what the painting depicted. The man had a bloodied knife clenched between his teeth. Red ran over his lips and dripped off his chin. More blood coated the front of his grey flannel shirt and had smeared up to his elbows. He looked victorious, energised… and *ecstatic*, as though his whole reason for living centred on the gore dribbling over his tongue.

Sam felt as though she might be sick. She'd tried her hand at a lot of styles while practicing her art, but she'd never created anything so violent. She turned away, struggling to breathe.

More paintings stood propped against the furniture, all facing Sam. It was an onslaught of images: a shadowed shape barely visible between dense trees. The man, his pose stiff and somehow unnatural, stood at the end of the dock—*Peter's dock*—and watched the rippling water below. A single finger, detached from its hand, rested on the forest floor.

Sam couldn't bring herself to look at the rest. The paintings all showed frank, unrestrained violence. And the sallow, grey-eyed man loved it all.

Sam stumbled to the sink and gagged, but nothing came up. Her mind felt choked and frantic. She'd never dealt well with gore. She couldn't believe her subconscious was creating those scenes.

The fire spat, shaking Sam from her stupor, and she raised her head from the sink as she became aware of her surroundings.

The pot sat on the bench, empty except for the dregs of the minestrone soup. *Did I eat it while I was asleep?* Behind her, the fire crackled, having been fed recently. She must have tended to it for hours while she created the paintings. And to her left, a single empty mug stood on the bench, its handle directed towards the canvas.

First three, then two, now just one. It's almost like a countdown.

She couldn't stand looking at the paintings, so she moved through the room and turned each of them around. Including the four she'd created previously, there were nine in total. *Just how long did I spend painting?*

It was pitch-dark outside the window. Sam guessed it was somewhere between three and four in the morning, which meant it would be at least three hours until dawn showed over the tops of the mountains.

A bleating, wailing noise cut through the night air. Sam jumped and turned towards the door. *It's just an animal. We're in the middle of a forest, remember.*

The noise had sounded close—almost as though it had come from the lake. Sam had never heard a sound like that before; there had been something unnatural about the way it hung in the frosty air, almost as if it were filled with notes of grief.

I need more light.

Only one candle still burned, placed beside the canvas to provide light for her work. Between the nearly melted nub of wax and the fire, about half of the room was lit. Shadows filled the rest.

Peter left a torch, didn't he?

Sam opened the cupboard where she'd found the radio. Sitting near the back, beside a stack of spare batteries, was a large halogen torch. Sam turned it on. Its light, a brilliant white, was much cooler than the glow from the fire, and the beam cut through the darkness beautifully.

Sam crossed the room in five paces and undid the front door's latch. She was trembling, almost uncontrollably, as she nudged the wood and glanced outside.

The ground immediately in front of the cabin was empty, so Sam pressed the door open farther. The air stung her nose and cheeks. She raised the torch, passing it over the slope leading to the lake, then swung it across the shore in both directions. Mist had developed, but it wasn't yet thick enough to block her view. The shore was empty.

Sam turned the torch on the dock, and her heart fluttered like a trapped bird. At the end of the pier, clear in the torch's light, knelt the man.

His back formed a severe curve as he sat on his haunches, hands clasped on the edge of the dock, and stared into the water. Sam thought he looked a little thicker than he did in the paintings, though it was hard to tell when he was hunched over. His hair was longer, too; it hung around his face like a limp curtain.

The man's shoulders trembled, and his spine, deeply exaggerated, poked against his skin and dark shirt. Sam inhaled sharply, then clamped a hand over her mouth. No healthy human's back looked that desperately skeletal.

The man heard. He shouldn't have been able to at that distance, but he had. He swivelled his head to stare at Sam, and the light reflected off his eyes, making them glint like a cat's. Then he began to move, oddly, like an insect. Each limb twisted in an unnatural motion as he lurched forward, scuttling to the edge of the dock. Over the edge. *Under* the dock.

Sam collapsed to her knees as the scene branded itself into her mind. The man had lurched over the edge of the pier, reached one bizarrely long arm forward, and somehow grasped the underside of the wood. The rest of his body had followed smoothly, effortlessly, and he disappeared underneath, like a spider hiding from an intrusive stranger.

That's it, her mind gibbered. *I'm done. Hang the Heritage and hang Peter's generosity. I'm not staying a second longer.*

Sam sucked in a shaking breath and dashed into her cabin. She scrambled through the messy table until she found the car keys, then she ran back outside, waving her torch in erratic arcs to ward off the shadows. Her mind felt blank, as though it were incapable of processing what she'd just seen. All she cared about was getting to a road with actual streetlamps and houses. Her clothes and art supplies could stay in the cabin. *I'll come back for them another time, when it's broad daylight and I'm accompanied by the police or the FBI or whoever's in charge of dealing with weird stuff.*

The car was waiting for her in front of the shed. Sam skidded to a halt beside it and shone her torch through the windows to make sure the interior was empty then threw herself inside. She didn't realise how badly she was shaking until she slammed the door and found herself incapable of fitting the key into the ignition. Sam closed her eyes, leaned her forehead against the steering wheel, and took long, slow gulps of air. The vicelike sensation around her chest gradually loosened as her nerves calmed, and she slotted the key into the ignition.

Good. Let's get the hell out of here.

Sam turned the key, but the motor failed to turn over. She bit at the inside of her check as fresh terror crawled up her spine.

No," she muttered, trying to control her breathing,

and turned the key again. Then a third, fourth and fifth time. The car wouldn't start.

The motor's cold, that's all, she told herself, even though she knew it wasn't true. The car had never failed her before, not even when it snowed.

She tried again. The car's motor churned but failed to tick over. "Come on, come on, *come on*."

Sam sat for a moment then turned her torch to the windows. The glass was fogging up, but she was alone as far as she could tell. She pressed the button to release the hood and scrambled out of the door, her heart thundering as she rounded the car to check its engine.

The problem was immediately obvious: someone had cut the fuel line—not just cut it, but cut it *twice*—and pulled the loose section of piping out to lay it neatly on top of the motor.

Someone doesn't want me to leave.

Instinct told her to turn off the torch, so she did. The only light came from the moon, which hung near one of the higher mountains, and the golden glow from inside the cabin.

Sam tried to calm her panicked mind and think through her options. Brandon would help her, she was sure, but the ranger's office was certainly closed at four in the morning. She had a two-way radio and codes to contact the police and emergency rescue team, though. They would take hours to reach her, but it was better than nothing.

Sam cast a final wary glance at the dock then began to slink towards the cabin. *I'll be safe inside, at least. I can lock the door, and I'll have the axe, and—*

Motion inside the cabin made her freeze. There was a silhouette—a man's silhouette—barely visible in the window closest to the door. He swayed slightly as he faced the cabin's entrance. He must have gotten into her cabin while she struggled with the car, and he was waiting patiently. *Waiting for me.*

Panic boiled over into full-blown terror. Sam crept backwards, towards the forest, keeping her body low and staying within the shed's shadows in case the man looked in her direction. When she reached the edge of the woods, she turned and ran.

CHAPTER 12

Sam's lungs burnt, and every muscle in her legs ached as she forced herself up the incline at a blistering pace. Every few minutes, she paused and held her breath, listening to the forest for signs that she might have been followed. There were none. *Not so far.*

She'd had to choose between keeping to the paths or striking out into the woods. She would be harder to find in the forest, but also in greater danger of becoming lost and turning into another victim of Trail T-1. She kept to the paths.

Sam had no idea who, or *what*, had been inside the

cabin, but she was certain she didn't want it following her. Whether Uncle Earnest had been right about the poltergeist or not, the thing in her cabin had almost certainly cut her fuel line and had been hiding in the corner of the room that would be hidden from view of anyone opening the door.

A torch in the dark night would stand out like a beacon, so Sam kept her light off. The moonlight penetrated the trees in sparse splotches, offering just enough light to find her way. The light was not quite enough to save her shins from being barked and her arms from being snagged and scratched by the vines, though.

She rested only once, when she reached the clump of rocks halfway up the hill. She collapsed onto one of the stones and dragged in thick, sticky breaths as she listened to the forest; rustling trees, bats, insects, frogs, and even the occasional small mammal competed for her attention. She heard no human sounds, though, which she was immensely grateful for.

The ground looked lighter up ahead, and Sam pressed forward, ignoring the stitch in her side and the way sweat stuck her shirt to her body, despite the cold air. She pushed through another patch of weeds and finally broke onto the main path. *Trail T-1.*

She turned right, towards the clearing that held the map. The ranger's office wouldn't be open, but Sam was banking on the idea that her stalker wouldn't expect her to go there, and she could wait by the front door for the morning shift to arrive. *It's not that far from dawn, anyway. This'll be fine. We'll be fine.*

Sam half-walked, half-jogged down the trail. It felt endless. Just when she was beginning to panic that she'd taken a bad turn and was on a completely wrong path, she nearly tripped over the chain barrier. She let her breath out in a hoarse cheer and ducked under the blockade.

Visibility was much better in the clearing. She increased her speed, ignoring her aching legs and thundering heart in her eagerness to reach the sign.

"Okay," Sam whispered, turning her light to examine the large map. "Okay, this is good. We're good. Let's find the ranger's office and get out of this place."

She started with the You Are Here tag and circled out. She found landmarks, lookouts, and intersections, but not the office. Sam's heart dropped as her circles became wider and wider.

"Damn it, where are you?"

She turned her torch towards the symbols key in the map's corner. A tree shape represented noteworthy plants, a sun hovering over a ledge was for lookouts, and exclamation points indicated difficult sections. Nothing for the ranger's office.

"No, no, no, *no, no.*"

Sam took a step back and turned her light across the board again. *It's got to be somewhere!*

Then she saw it: a note at the base of the map, written in neat block.

Need emergency help? Rangers patrol these woods during the day. The park office is located at the entrance to the park, on the corner of Harob Forest Road and Mindy Lane.

"The entrance to the park…"

Sam slumped against the sign and cradled her head in her hands. The entrance was a full two hours' drive away. *How long would it take me to walk?*

If she'd brought her walkie-talkie, she'd have been able to call for help. But of course, she hadn't; she'd left it nestled amongst her art supplies in the cabin, which was playing host to a stranger.

And it wasn't just the walkie-talkie that was missing. She was desperately thirsty, but had no water. More, she wore only her light jacket, and the night chill was seeping through the thin fabric, making her shiver. It would get worse closer to dawn.

I've got no choice except to return to the cabin… or freeze to death in the forest.

She sat for a moment, basking in the noises of the night. Tears leaked out of the corners of her eyes, but she didn't brush them away. Instead, she pulled herself to her feet, swallowed the metallic taste that had developed in her mouth, and turned to the cordoned-off trail.

"You've got to be strong, Sammy," her mother had whispered during those last few hours on her deathbed. Her voice had rasped horribly as her eyes stared, unfocussed, at the off-white ceiling. Sam had squeezed her hand, but her mother didn't seem to feel it. *"You're going to have to face a lot of things without me. Be strong, like I know you are. Be brave."*

"Be strong," Sam echoed, forcing her feet to move her body onto the trail leading to the dock, the sabotaged car, and the *thing* waiting for her. "Be brave."

CHAPTER 13

Thirst became an increasingly pressing issue as Sam retraced her path through the woods. She tried to ignore it, but the hike had left her mouth dry, and her head was starting to pound.

I should be passing the rockslide soon. Then it's just another hour—or a bit more—to the cabin. And maybe the thing inside the cabin's moved on by now. Maybe it'll be safe again.

She stumbled over branches and rocks, staggered through a clump of vines, and hesitated. *I don't remember the path being this choked on the way up. I haven't taken a wrong turn, have I?*

Sam paused and turned in a semi-circle. Nothing looked familiar… not that unfamiliarity meant anything. She wouldn't have recognised anything except major landmarks, and there weren't many of those in her part of the forest. The path definitely seemed narrower and more cluttered than she remembered it, though.

Keep calm, Sam told herself as anxiety began to rise in her. *This whole place is like a giant bowl. As long as you're walking downhill, you'll reach the lake eventually, then you can just follow the beach until you find the cabin.*

She wasn't sure if she was imagining it or not, but she thought the sky was in the early stages of dawn. There was definitely some sort of light ahead, at least.

Wait… that's not natural light.

Sam squinted through the trees at the faint, flickering glow. *Is it the cabin? Did I find my way back by accident?* Her heart rose for a second before she tamped down the excitement. *No, that's impossible. I'm still a long way from the beach.*

And yet, something was glowing through the trees like a beacon. Sam moved forward, fighting through the tangled growth, and found herself in a clearing.

Ahead stood a cabin. It was worlds away from the tidy, orderly house Peter had lent her. Squat and dark, it looked as though it had been constructed by hand, then repeatedly repaired and patched as it slowly broke down. A tarpaulin was strapped over one side of the roof, and the windows had no glass.

Behind the cabin, in a tangled vegetable patch, weeds fought the tomato plants for dominance. Beyond that was a makeshift hutch that, judging by the faint clucking sounds, housed fowl. The light Sam had seen was coming from the cabin's window, where a single candle flickered on the sill.

Prudence told her to turn around and disappear back into the forest. Necessity, though, was far more insistent. *If there's a house, there'll be water.*

Sam hesitated for just a second before stepping out from the shadows of the trees. She didn't like the cabin's appearance, but it seemed empty, and she was in no position to reject a chance to drink. *Especially if I'm lost. I have no idea how long it might take me to get back to the lake.*

One of the fowl fluttered inside the enclosure, and Sam jumped. The bird didn't look like any sort of domestic hen or duck, so Sam guessed it might be a wild bird.

Who could possibly live here? They can't have permission from the government, surely, or they would have built their cabin by the lake like Peter did. It couldn't be someone on the run from the law, could it? Or... is it related to that thing at the lake?

Sam approached the door. She was almost completely certain the cabin was empty, but that didn't stop her from calling, "Hello?"

Only the very faint ticking of a clock answered.

Sam glanced behind herself, where the clearing was still and dark, and then, ignoring the anxious palpitations in her chest, she pushed on the cabin's door.

The cabin's single room looked a lot like the outside: well used and slowly falling apart. A layer of compact dirt covered the floor. The furniture—a table, a single chair, and a large collection of oddly shaped shelves—appeared hand-made and took up most of the room. A brick fireplace stood in the corner. Unlike Peter's fireplace, it was small, grimy, and looked frequently used.

Trinkets and knickknacks covered the shelves, ranging from compasses and maps to melamine bowls, crockery, a mug that smelt faintly of whisky, an old-fashioned clock, and a stack of mismatched cloths.

Sparkling silver caught Sam's attention, and she turned to see a board hung above the table. Two dozen nails had been crudely hammered into the wood, and from each one hung a knife.

Some were small—just paring knives, no larger than the ones Peter kept in his kitchen drawers—but others were long and serrated. Two were butchers knives. The bench below them was stained red.

Nausea grew in Sam's stomach. She staggered

backwards and bumped into something leaning against the wall; turning, she saw a row of axes and a chainsaw.

Calm down, Sam told herself, as cold sweat built across her body. *This house belongs to someone living in the woods. Of course he'd have to catch and kill his own food. It's nothing abnormal.*

There're so many knives, though. At least twenty. Surely one person doesn't need twenty.

Sam squeezed her hands into fists as she rotated on the spot. The anxious feeling in her chest was exploding into terror.

"Calm down, calm down, calm down," she muttered to herself, willing her mind to unfreeze. "Just find the water and get out."

There was no kitchen, tap, or sink. A large bowl sat on the bench, half-filled with liquid, but Sam cringed away from it. She had no idea if it was drinking water, used for bathing, or something else.

There's got to be clean water somewhere.

A cupboard near the fireplace caught her eye. It was the only storage unit with doors, which made it look like a kitchen pantry. Sam pulled open the doors.

Unlabelled bottles crowded the shelves. Some looked as though they were full of jams. Others seemed to contain pickled vegetables. Two held some type of dried meat jerky, and others were full of a brown-tinted liquid that she suspected was alcohol.

Behind everything else was a stack of water bottles.

There were close to fifty of them. Most of the seals were broken, and they had clearly been refilled multiple times, but Sam spotted a small cluster of unopened bottles near the back and took one.

She pushed the rest of the jars back into place and reached for the cupboard's handles to close the doors, but she hesitated. Another row of containers stood on the highest shelf, lined up far more neatly then the bottles below them. They each had one small, long item floating in clear liquid.

Curiosity got the better of Sam. She shoved the bottle of water into her jacket pocket then took one of the jars.

Floating inside, gently bouncing off the glass walls, was a woman's finger.

A horrified gurgle escaped Sam's throat, and she shoved the container back onto the shelf. The jars each held a single finger. All index fingers. All from different hands.

She couldn't tear her eyes away from the horrific sight. There were so many types of fingers—slender and feminine, gnarled, stubbly, or wrinkled—all preserved with care.

Sounds filtered through Sam's panic, and she became aware of leaves crunching and twigs snapping as someone moved through the forest. Sam turned towards the window that overlooked the path she'd come down.

It looks familiar, somehow…

Fresh adrenaline shot through her as she recognised the scene. She was horribly familiar with the sick, twisted trees lining the dirt path. *It's the image from my painting. Any second, the grey-eyed man's going to come into view, carrying an axe as he returns home—*

A figure was materialising out of the darkness, catching faint glints of moonlight as he moved into view. Sam shrunk away from the window, barely daring to breathe as she searched for an escape. The door faced the man's path, making it impossible to slip outside without attracting his attention. But there was nowhere to hide inside the one-room cabin.

The footsteps grew closer. Sam's eyes landed on the window at the opposite side of the room, and seizing the only option available to her, she clambered onto the bloodied bench and slid over the sill.

She misjudged the size of the window and fell into the bushes outside with a muffled *whump*. She thought the footsteps paused for a moment, as though the man had heard her. Then his pace increased, and the cabin's door was pulled open.

Sam tried to shrink into a ball and squeezed her eyes closed, hoping the spindly bushes would conceal her. She heard the man walk through his cabin, slowly and ponderously, then come to a halt not far from the window.

A horrible realisation hit Sam, and her stomach dropped. *I didn't close the cupboard doors.*

The cabin's entrance opened with a bang. Sam shrunk farther into the bushes, aware that their patchy branches did a poor job of masking her. The footsteps drew closer, coming down the side of the cabin, and Sam held her breath, squeezing her shaking hands into fists, as her stalker rounded the house and came into view.

The moonlight hit his face as he paused barely ten feet from her hiding spot, and she saw the familiar grey eyes, the salt-and-pepper stubble, and the vicious, healing scar on his cheek.

Just like in the paintings. They're so accurate that I could have been creating them from a photo.

The man scanned the woods behind his cabin. Sam didn't dare inhale, even though her lungs ached and her head throbbed. Her heartbeat was loud in her ears, and she felt certain that the man would be able to hear it. He wasn't looking in her direction, though, but faced the forest. Sam caught a brief glimpse of an axe—*uncle Peter's axe*—clasped in his hand before the man stepped towards the trees and disappeared between them with unexpected litheness.

CHAPTER 14

Sam didn't move for a long time. Her heart beat frantically, and she struggled to draw breath. Even though the forest was still, she kept imagining she heard footsteps heralding the man's return.

Gotta get moving, Sam. Get to your feet. Get away from his house.

Movement seemed impossible, though. Her limbs were locked up with terror, and her body couldn't draw in oxygen quickly enough. Then a fat, heavy insect landed on Sam's face and broke the trance. She jolted to her feet, fighting her way out from the bushes, and staggered through the clearing. One of the fowls squawked in alarm as she passed the hutch. Sam glanced behind herself once, searching between the trees, but the only movement came from the trembling leaves. She turned towards the woods that would lead in the direction opposite to the way the man had taken.

Terror had given her strength, and Sam ran as quickly and as silently as the dense woods would allow her to. She didn't dare turn her torch back on. Instead, she held both hands ahead of herself to protect her face from the worst of the scratching branches and focussed on moving her feet in long, careful strides. She didn't know which direction she was going, but she didn't care. All she wanted was to be away from the strange cabin and away from the man, to keep him from adding any of her fingers to his sick collection.

The woods cleared, and Sam stumbled to a halt on the edge of a drop-off. Her legs were weak, and her lungs ached, so she let herself slump onto the rocks to rest. Dehydration taxed her body, setting up a pounding headache behind her eyes. Remembering she'd pocketed the bottle of water, Sam felt for it in her jacket. To her surprise and relief, the bottle had survived her fall out of the window. She tugged the cap off and drained it.

Dawn was still at least half an hour away, and the

moon bathed the area in its pale light. Trees coated the slope ahead of Sam, which dipped until it met the lake. Dense fog hid the water from sight. Sam thought she saw a faint glow on the beach. *Peter's cabin. Should I be going back there?*

I don't think I have a choice.

As soon as she'd stopped moving, the cold had begun biting at her in earnest. She didn't have nearly enough layers, and she knew the temperature would continue to drop until dawn broke.

Besides, there's the radio in the cabin. If I go inside for just a minute to grab the radio, the codes, some water, and my heavier jacket, at least I'll have a proper chance of getting out of here.

With any luck, Sam thought, the man would either still be searching the woods or have returned to his cabin to check that nothing had been stolen. Sam didn't think he would wait for her in Peter's house a second time.

She crumpled the empty water bottle and tucked it inside her pocket before climbing to her aching legs. She'd found her way to one of the steeper parts of the mountain and had to slow to a crawl to climb down the cliffs to the shore.

A hint of light dissolved the stars near the opposite side of the lake as the sun started its daily climb over the mountain ridge. The cold increased as Sam moved lower. By the time she stumbled onto the beach, uncontrollable shivers wracked her. She didn't dare remove her hands from where she'd tucked them inside her jacket, even though the condensed fog dripped from her nose. The cabin's fire, burnt down to embers, provided a faint glow to guide her to the cabin.

Sam slowed her pace as she drew closer, glancing between the dock and the cabin. It was hard to see through the mist, but both seemed deserted. Sam was too close to exhaustion to give the situation as much caution as she knew it deserved, and she only paused to glance through the cabin's window and check the room was empty before pushing inside.

The difference in temperature was amazing, and Sam sucked a deep breath of warm air into her lungs. She knew she couldn't stay long, but she dared to take a moment to hold her icy fingers over the embers.

As she warmed her hands, Sam took a quick assessment of the cabin. The paintings were exactly where she'd left them, facing the walls. The axe was missing from beside the fireplace, though, and Sam didn't like the way that made her feel.

The cabin seemed still and quiet. As soon as feeling returned to her fingers, Sam went to the kitchen sink and took one of the small paring knives out of the drawer then moved to the cupboard to get the radio.

"What..."

The radio was also gone. Sam glanced around the room, hoping she'd forgotten to put it away, but it was missing. *No, not missing. Taken. He wanted me to be completely stranded. No car, no phone, no radio...*

"The walkie-talkie!"

Sam crossed to the table. Its surface was covered with papers and art supplies, and Sam dug through them until she found the black box hidden near the back, where she'd tossed it after the less-than-helpful talk with the female ranger. Sam tried to guess the time; judging by the light that was bleeding across the outside sky, it had to be after six but before seven. *What time do the rangers come in?*

She pressed the button and said, "Hello?"

A prolonged crackle answered her, then a click and a man's voice, sounding half-asleep, replied, "Yeah, hello, this is the ranger's office. How can I be of assistance?"

Sam closed her eyes and drew in a relieved breath. The voice was familiar. She pressed the button again and tried to keep her hands from shaking. "Hi, this is Sam. I'm staying at the cabin by the lake. A strange man's stalking me, and I think he might be responsible for the missing hikers."

CHAPTER 15

"Sam!" a sharp note filled the voice, cutting through its tiredness. "This is Brandon. We met the other day. Tell me exactly what happened."

Sam did, in stumbling and confused fragments. The panicky, sleepless night was catching up to her. She knew she wasn't making as much sense as she should have, but Brandon interrupted only twice, to clarify the order of events. She told him about her car cables being cut, seeing a figure inside her cabin, and discovering the shanty in the woods. She expected him to laugh at the part where she'd found the fingers preserved in jars, but he didn't. The only part of the story Sam didn't share was seeing the figure at the end of the dock. *That's too fantastical for anyone to believe.*

When Sam finished, she held her breath and waited for Brandon's response. He didn't say anything for a moment, and she tried to imagine his face. *Is he laughing at me? Does he think it's a prank, maybe, or that I'm delusional?*

But then he spoke, and her fears melted away. He sounded anxious, but maintained a well-practiced note of authority in his voice. "Sam, are you somewhere safe?"

"Uh… I think so." Sam glanced around the cabin. She hadn't searched the upstairs room, but it had been completely silent since her arrival. "I'm in the cabin."

"Have you locked the door?"

Sam crossed the room and pulled the bolt. "I have now."

"Do you have a weapon?"

"I've got a small knife."

"That's better than nothing," Brandon said. "Sam, the first thing I want you to do is ensure you're safe. Search the cabin. I'm going to drive down there to pick you up. It'll take a bit over an hour, so the priority right now is to make sure you're not in danger."

Sam was already moving through the cabin,

searching in any and every crevice a human could possibly fit. She opened each of the downstairs cupboards then moved upstairs, walkie-talkie in one hand and knife in the other, to search the bedroom. It was empty.

"Okay, I'm definitely alone."

"Good. Keep the door locked, and make sure you've got the knife and walkie-talkie with you at all times. I'm on my way, but if you see or hear anything, let me know immediately."

"Will do."

"See you soon, Sam."

The line went quiet, and Sam released a long breath. She approached the doors overlooking the balcony, and gazed through the glass windows.

The sun had finally breached the top of the mountains and begun to spread its glow across the lake. The mist was still dense, but seemed to be clearing.

Sam weighed her options. Brandon seemed to think she should stay in the cabin. On one hand, it was at least somewhat defensible. On the other, it would be easy for the grey-eyed man to find her there.

She took the stairs back to the ground floor and gazed at the paintings propped against the furniture and walls.

There was so much she didn't understand. Why had she been painting the images? How had she known the man's face before ever seeing it? She knew there were clues somewhere, possibly even hidden in the images, but she was just being too obtuse to notice them.

She didn't want to look at the paintings again, but a desperate need to *understand* compelled her to turn them around one at a time.

First was the painting of the man standing on the crop of rocks overlooking the lake. It was a replica of what she'd seen while on the lake, though she didn't know how her asleep-self had guessed his face. The second painting was of water, swirling and frantic— another echo of her canoeing experience. *At least, I think it is. I fell into weedy, muddy water, but the painting is clear and blue.*

She turned over the third image and grimaced at the sight of the man crouched over his victim, blood dripping down his chin from the knife he'd clasped between his teeth. The one after that depicted a single bloodied finger lying amongst the leaves. *Almost like I'd known what he did to his victims. But that should be impossible.*

Next was a glimpse of the man between dense trees then one of him running towards the viewer, a long, serrated knife gripped in his fist, a vicious smile spread across his face.

Following that, she turned the painting of the grey-eyed man striding down the path leading to his home.

Again, Sam had to face the idea that her mind had been showing her images before they'd happened. The appearance of the gnarled, sickened trees lining the path, the axe clasped in his hand, and even the way he looked—only faintly visible amongst the shadows—were true to Sam's experience just hours before.

Then she turned another painting, one she hadn't looked at the day before, and saw a bottle of clear liquid with a woman's finger floating in it. Sam's stomach flipped, and she looked away.

After that came the first image she'd created: the close-up of the man's face. The salt-and-pepper hair, the stubble, the grey eyes, and the red scar on his cheek were all so familiar. She'd thought when she'd first seen it that it was a face she'd known before — but she was no closer to remembering from where.

The final painting showed the man standing on the edge of the dock, watching the water intently. Sam found herself transfixed by it. She felt that if she could only see what the grey-eyed man was seeing, she would have answers.

There's something in the water he can't stay away from. He's been coming back to the cabin almost every day since I've been here, just to look into the lake.

Sam remembered the way he'd crawled over the edge of the dock, moving to hide underneath it like a giant insect, and couldn't stop shudders from creeping down her spine. *That wasn't human. No way, no how. Does that mean Uncle Earnest was right? Is he some sort of vengeful spirit? A poltergeist?*

She thought back to the cabin, with its bottles of water, jars of food, vegetable garden, and poultry—all things a human needed.

And yet… I couldn't have imagined seeing him crawl under the dock, could I? I'd not long woken up from a concussion, but even so, it was too clear and too real to be a hallucination. If only I could look over the edge… if only I could see…

Sam had walked towards the front door without realising it, and she stopped herself with one hand on the bolt. She shook her head, trying to dispel the tiredness that was fogging her mind.

Nope. No. Definitely not. We're not going outside. We're not setting so much as a toe on that dock. It would be insanity.

Sam turned back to the room. The paintings surrounded her, smothering her in their portent. Her eyes fell on the image of the man leaning over the dock and watching the water. He looked so focussed—obsessed, even.

It's too cold to stay outdoors for long, so the man probably won't come back until later today, if at all. And Brandon will be here in an hour. This could be my only chance to see what he sees. To understand.

"What the hell," Sam said, and unbolted the door. "It's hardly the craziest thing I've done this week."

She paused on the threshold and gazed up and

down the length of the shore. The canoe, empty, still rested on the dirt, one end barely dipped into the water. The mountain's trees rippled as a breeze tugged at their branches. The mist was gone. Dark clouds clustered over the sky, threatening rain. The cold air bit at Sam's nose and cheeks, but it no longer had the cruel edge she'd felt when walking home.

Sam closed the door behind herself and moved towards the dock. Its supports, still damp from the mist, stood out against the crystalline water. Hyper-aware, she approached the lake. Every birdcall and rustle of the tree branches seemed to hold potential danger, and Sam kept her eyes roving over her surroundings. Instead of stepping onto the dock, she followed the ground's gentle slope until the edge of the lake lapped at her sneakers, then knelt to look under the pier.

There were no dark, hulking shapes lurking underneath or glowing red eyes watching her. Sam let her breath out, swallowed the lump in her throat, and moved back until she could climb onto the dock. The first slat creaked under her feet, and she hesitated.

Don't chicken out now. This is what you wanted, isn't it?

Sam narrowed her eyes, squared her shoulders, and began to move down the dock, testing each step before she dared place her weight on it. Her breath caught every time the wood groaned.

Her limbs were trembling by the time she reached

the dock's end, and she lowered herself to her knees, one hand on the support. She couldn't stop herself from imagining how she must look from the shore; crouched over the end of the dock, she would be an almost perfect replica of the man who'd haunted her stay at the lake.

Shaking fingers gripped the edge of the wood as Sam leant forward, extending her torso over the lip of the dock, to look into the water below.

CHAPTER 16

At first, she saw only her own reflection, her anxiety-widened eyes set in pale skin. Then she looked past the water's surface and saw what had captivated the man so much.

"Oh," Sam said simply, as revulsion and horror rose through her chest and threatened to choke her.

Suspended in the water, only a foot below the surface, floated a man's body. The white face was turned towards her, its empty eye sockets staring blindly. Sam could see into the open mouth: the tongue was gone—devoured—and white teeth poked out of shrunken gums. The corpse's skin was frayed and pocked with holes where decay and water creatures had eaten through the flesh. Shoulder-length bronze hair washed around the head, making a gently swaying halo.

Sam felt frozen in place, unable to release her grip on the edge of the dock and incapable of looking away. The body's limbs were intact; its limp arms were spread out and had become tangled in the thick weeds. Her eyes turned to the figure's right hand, which was missing a finger.

A strangled, horrified noise escaped Sam's throat. She wrenched herself backwards, away from the body in the water, and stumbled upright. Her chest had constricted, and panic set her fingers shaking. She turned and began running towards the shore.

One of the dock's beams splintered under her feet, and Sam threw herself forward to avoid falling through the hole. She hit the dock hard, knocking the wind out of her lungs, and her vision swam.

She rolled onto her back, trying to smother the groans of fear and pain that escaped between her clenched teeth, and looked towards the end of the dock.

A pale hand stretched up, over the lip of the pier, and slapped onto the wooden edge, sending a spray of water ahead of it. Sam opened her mouth to scream, but the sound died as a gurgle in her throat. A second hand emerged from the water, reaching forward and smacking onto the wood in front of the first, and then the muscles in the arms flexed as they began pulling the body out of the lake.

The head emerged, raining water, its empty eye sockets focussed on Sam, its mouth open to expose the rotting gums and white teeth.

Sam turned and threw herself down the dock, no longer caring if the wood gave out under her feet. She could hear the cadaver dragging itself onto the dock. Its nails scratched at the wood. The water that dripped from it made quiet tapping noises. Then the being exhaled, expelling the liquid from its lungs, and drew a raspy, laborious breath.

Sam reached the end of the dock and turned towards the cabin, adrenaline powering her aching legs, her lungs fighting to bring in enough oxygen to support the exertion. She didn't stop moving until her hands had fixed around the cabin's metal doorhandle and wrenched it open.

She turned on the cabin's threshold, prepared to slam the door if the horror had followed her, but the dock was empty.

"What... *what on earth...*"

Sam clung to the wooden doorframe, her eyes scanning the shore, the trees, the dock, and the lake. Struggling to draw breath, she felt dizzy and nauseated, and her head throbbed. She didn't think her legs would hold her weight for much longer. No shapes appeared out of the water, so she closed and bolted the door.

There are two men, Sam realised with sickening horror. *I've been trying to hide from a single person, but there are actually two of them. The grey-eyed man, and…* that.

It was mercifully quiet inside the cabin. Sam cast a glance at the paintings spaced around the room, then she grabbed the walkie-talkie from the table and stumbled towards the stairs. *The bedroom's balcony has the best view out of anywhere in the cabin.*

Sam's body felt leaden as she climbed the stairs. When she reached the bedroom, she opened the balcony doors and settled on the edge of the bed, which was close enough to the balcony to allow her to watch the dock.

How long until Brandon gets here? Forty minutes? Half an hour?

Sam rubbed at her aching eyes. Everything hurt, from her pounding head to her dry mouth to her shaking legs. *At least it's warmer in the cabin's upper level.* Sam scooted farther back onto the bed and pulled the quilt around herself. It was soft, familiar, and safe, and she sighed as she nestled into it.

The minutes ticked by slowly as she stared out over the balcony, her eyes fixed on the dark pier, and the tension gradually left her limbs. As the immediate edge of panic faded, exhaustion set in; she'd barely slept the previous night, and she was drained both physically and emotionally. She felt dazed and dull. The bird calls filtering through the open balcony doors were pleasantly repetitive and comforting. She watched as the last shreds of mist dissipated, leaving the lake clear and smooth. The sky was starting to darken with heavy clouds, though. *We might be in for some rain later today.*

Sam didn't even realise her eyes were closing until she found herself falling backwards onto the bed, and by then it was too late to fight.

Her dream was rushed and indistinct. She saw herself painting. She was frantic with stress as she held a jar in one hand and copied its contents onto the canvas. Inside the jar was a finger… *no, not just anyone's finger—my finger.* The grey-eyed man owned it, and she had to paint it quickly, before he took it back, so she would never forget what it looked like. She couldn't get it right, though, and the people behind her were becoming agitated. They begged her to hurry. She was supposed to paint their fingers next, and they'd already been waiting such a long time. *Denzel will never forgive me if I don't deliver the fingers to the Heritage in time…*

Sam snapped awake, and her body revolted against

the abruptly interrupted sleep cycle. She couldn't immediately tell what had disturbed her. She was still on the bed, wrapped in the doona. The sky was clogged with dark clouds, and the balcony doors stood open, letting the chilled air in, though she didn't feel cold.

Then she became aware of the body behind her. It seemed so natural, lying beside her on the bed, its chest pressed to her back and its arm draped over her waist like a lover's.

But he wasn't alive. *Not anymore.*

He felt familiar, Sam realised, because she'd already met in. They'd been companions for days. He was the mind that had guided her hand while she slept, funnelling his memories into the paintings she'd so skilfully created. He'd taught her to recognise the grey-eyed man's face and shown her the deaths. He'd led her to set up the mugs as a crude countdown. And his was the figure she'd seen knelt on the edge of the dock, staring into the water day after day, as he watched over his final resting place.

Sam didn't dare move. He felt so human, and yet so *cold*, as he lay behind her, embracing her. It almost felt *normal*. Slowly, cautiously, Sam turned her head to look over her shoulder.

The two empty eyesockets stared back. His brow, where white bone peeked through the gaps in the flesh, was creased in concern for her. His lips opened then, and his voice was dry, raspy, and urgent.

"He's coming," the cadaver whispered. "Run."

CHAPTER 17

Sam launched herself out of the bed, a scream held at bay behind tightly squeezed lips. She hit the cabin's wall and turned to face the bed.

The corpse was gone.

Sam gasped. Her heart thundered as she rubbed her sweaty palms across her jeans. *A dream. It was just a dream. Calm down.*

And yet, there was a strange smell about the room, like dirty water and organic decay. It felt thick in Sam's lungs and was somehow familiar.

Sam swore under her breath. She snatched the

walkie-talkie off the bedside table and pressed the button. "Brandon, are you there? It's Sam."

The crackling static answered her. Sam waited for nearly a full minute then pressed the button again. "Brandon? Hello?"

She listened with increasing frustration to the background noise then paced to the balcony and looked outside. The sky was still dark and swirling, creating strange patterns on the water's surface. Sam tried to guess the time, but that was nearly impossible without the sun.

Then she heard the faint click of a closing door. Sam's heart froze, and she turned towards the stairs leading to the ground floor. She raised the walkie-talkie to her mouth and pressed the button.

"Brandon?" She didn't dare raise her voice above a whisper. "Please, please answer me. He's here."

The only reply was static.

Footsteps echoed through the floor below then stopped. Sam imagined the man standing in the centre of the room, his grey eyes scanning the myriad of paintings depicting him. *Would they confuse him? Disturb him, even?* Then the footsteps resumed, leading across the room and towards the stairwell.

Panic flooded her, lending her tired limbs strength. Sam cast around for some type of defence. She'd left the knife in the downstairs room, and there was no other weapon in the bedroom. *Nowhere to hide, either.*

The footsteps changed timbre as he began climbing the stairs. Sam clamped both hands over her mouth, trying to muffle her frantic breathing, as she searched with increasing desperation for some kind of rescue. Her eyes landed on the window.

Sam crossed to the balcony's bannister and looked over the edge. She hated how far away the ground seemed, but there was no time left to find any other option. She swung her leg over the wooden barrier, and her heart jumped as the wood swayed under her weight. The footsteps were nearly at the top of the stairs.

There's no time. Do it now!

She dropped over the outside of the bannister and lowered herself until her hands clung to the wooden struts and her legs dangled over the drop.

The man appeared at the top of the stairs. His wild, steel-grey eyes fixed on Sam for a split second before she let go.

Impact forced Sam's breath from her as she hit the ground. Pain shot up her right leg, and, for a moment of blind panic, she thought she might have broken it. It still moved, though, and could take enough weight to let her scramble on her back away from the foot of the cabin.

The man stood on the balcony, his bony hands gripping the rail she'd just released. Sam hadn't realised before just how tall he was; he seemed to fill the entire doorway, and sinewy muscles bulged under his dirty shirt. He had a rope coil slung around one shoulder, and she thought she saw the edge of the axe under his dark moleskin coat.

Sam stared, transfixed, at the furious grey eyes that had haunted her. *They seem so much more malevolent in the flesh.*

The man's lip curled into a sneer, and he turned back to the room. He wasn't reckless or desperate enough to follow her over the bannister, which meant the climb down the stairs would buy Sam a few seconds.

A few seconds for what? My car won't start, and there's not enough time to hide.

Sam scrambled to her feet, wincing as pain flashed up her injured leg. She turned in a semi-circle, searching for an escape, and caught sight of a dark car parked twenty meters away, near the path that led towards the entrance to the park. Its driver door stood open.

Did the grey-eyed man drive here? I didn't see a car on his property, but that doesn't mean he didn't have one. If he left the keys in the ignition…

No matter how repulsive she found the idea of touching his property, Sam knew she couldn't reject the only lifeline offered to her. She made for the car as quickly as she could, gritting her teeth against the pain stabbing through her leg.

She'd nearly reached the vehicle when she caught sight of the emblem emblazoned on the door. *Harob Park Ranger's Office.*

"Brandon…" Sam threw herself towards the driver's side.

The ranger lay slumped across the steering wheel, one hand thrown over the dash, the other lying limply in his lap. His face was turned towards the door as his dark eyes gazed sightlessly out of ashen skin and his mouth hung open in an expression of surprise.

"Brandon!" Sam pulled open the door and shook the ranger's arm. He slid a few inches sideways before catching in his locked seatbelt. Something dark protruded from his back. Sam's hands fluttered towards it, but she couldn't bring herself to touch the knife embedded between the man's shoulder blades. "No, no, no, please, no—"

She turned to face the cabin, forest, and lake as she fought to draw breath. She couldn't see the man. *Is he still inside the cabin? In the woods? Why hasn't he followed me?*

The answer came easily. *I have no way to escape. He knows he can take his time stalking me. That's what this is for him—a hunt… and he doesn't want it to end too quickly.*

Sam turned back to the car and brushed Brandon's chocolate hair away from his face with shaking fingers. A sob stuck in her throat, but she pushed it back down and blinked to clear her eyes. *Focus. Find a way out.*

Sam looked in the ignition, hoping it might still hold the keys, but the man had taken them. She then leaned over Brandon's shoulder to look into the backseat.

A first-aid kit, an animal trap, a thick guidebook, spare boots, and a jacket were scattered about the back. If Brandon had brought any weapons, the man had taken them. A blanket lay crumpled on the car's floor behind the driver's seat, and Sam stared at it. That morning's events were slowly falling into place.

Brandon had said it would take him an hour to reach Sam, but the ranger's office was more than two hours away, at the entrance to the park. That meant he must have already been in the forest when Sam contacted him. He'd probably been checking the park's traps for animals to tag and monitor, if the cage in the back of the car was any indication.

Is it possible the grey-eyed man had a walkie-talkie? Or had he been near enough to Brandon to listen in on our conversation? If he'd heard us, and if he'd gotten to the car before Brandon did, it would have been all too easy to hide under the blanket in the backseat. He'd have an easy ride to the cabin before attacking his unknowing host.

Sam squeezed her eyes closed, fighting her grief and fear, and stepped back from the car. A spot of rain hit her arm. She turned in a semi-circle, fruitlessly searching for the man. *He'll be somewhere he can watch me without being seen. He wants to see what I'm going to do. What am I going to do? I could go into the cabin and get one of the paring knives out of the drawer… as though that would be any sort of defence against an axe. Or I could go into the forest and try to outrun him… but I'd have nowhere to go, and he's more familiar with the woods than I am. Or…*

Sam's eyes landed on the canoe, its tip barely dipped into the water. *There aren't any other boats. If I got onto the lake, he wouldn't be able to follow me.*

Thunder cracked overhead. Sam ran, moving her pained leg as fast as she could, towards the water's edge. She didn't let herself think about what she would do once she was on the water or how she hoped to escape from the forest; everything else was secondary to her immediate need to put as much distance as she could between herself and her stalker.

Sam was nearly at the canoe when the man burst from the forest's edge. He kept his body low and moved lithely as he arced towards her. She caught a glimpse of his eyes, manic with excitement, his hungry smile stretching the scar across his cheek. Then Sam's hands hit the canoe's end, and she shoved it into the water with all of her strength.

It was heavy and ground forward slowly. Sam poured every bit of adrenaline into the task, fighting against gravity and the boat, until it was waterborne and rushing across the lake's surface. Sam continued pushing it until the water reached her thighs, then hauled herself over the edge of the canoe. It nearly overbalanced, but Sam threw herself towards its opposite side to right it, then grabbed the paddle and plunged it into the water.

She glanced over her shoulder and saw that the man had paused on the edge of the lake. He held his head high, and a cruel delight stretched his lips into a grin.

Sam pulled the paddle through the water, and the canoe spun. She quickly changed sides, trying to temper her frantic energy to a more efficient level. She didn't dare look behind herself again, but she could hear the man moving; the dirt crunched under his boots as he paced along the shore. He was moving languidly—*confidently*—and Sam didn't like it. She focussed on drawing her paddle through the water, moving the canoe farther into the lake. Farther from *him*.

Thunder crashed again, and what had been gentle spits of water turned into a downpour.

The footsteps changed from a crunching noise to a quiet thud, accompanied by a strange scraping sound. Sam couldn't stop herself from looking, and icy-cold fear ran through her chest. The man was pacing down the length of the dock. He'd taken the rope off his shoulder, and a large grappling hook hung from its end, its edges viciously sharp. He let the metal hook drag along the slats to create the scraping sound that had set Sam's teeth on edge.

He thought I might use the canoe, and he came prepared.

Sam swore and pulled her paddle through the water too quickly, breaking the canoe's momentum and sending it into a spin. A muted whirring noise replaced the scraping. Sam moved the paddle to the other side of the boat, but overcompensated again, and her vessel lurched. Before she could correct it, a loud *clang* filled her ears, and she felt the boat rock as the grappling hook found its mark.

Sam turned to see the hook had landed inside the boat, but hadn't yet caught on the wood. Pure instinct took over and pushed her to fight. She dived towards the hook, intending to lift it and throw it overboard, but just as her hand tightened around the cold, curved metal, the man gave it a ferocious tug.

The force of the pull, combined with the boat's lurch, threw her off her feet. She hit the rain-dampened hull and screamed as the hook trapped her hand against the canoe's bow, crushing her fingers.

Sam's vision blurred as pain overrode her senses. Her fingers felt as though they'd been set on fire. She tried to get her spare hand behind the hook to pull it off, but her stalker gave an extra-sharp tug, increasing the pressure, and Sam cried out again.

The man stood on the edge of the dock, legs braced on the wood, both hands wrapped around the rope as he pulled her closer in long, easy drags. She couldn't look away. The wolfish, blood-hungry smile dominated his face, as his terrible grey eyes laughed at her while the rain drenched him. She would be at the edge of the dock in a few seconds. *What then? Will he use the axe or one of the knives? Will he take my finger before or after he kills me?*

She had no energy left to fight him or even to free her burning, trapped hand. Her eyes dropped and widened as movement underneath the dock caught her attention. Bodies were pulling themselves out of the weedy area below the pier, dripping water as they clung to the dark supports. *There's so many of them. Are they all his?*

Gaunt, sightless, decaying faces turned upwards, towards the dock, and sallow hands rose to dig their nails into the wood, applying their weight to the decaying structure. Even in the canoe, Sam could hear the scratching, scraping noises they produced. The man heard them, too, and his smile faltered as he glanced towards his feet. He was just in time to see the wood splinter below his boots, then the dock gave out, and he plunged through the hole and into the waiting arms of his victims.

CHAPTER 18

The pressure on the hook slackened, then the canoe bumped into the edge of the dock and rebounded. Sam was finally able to force her left hand under the hook. She pulled as hard as she could, digging it out of the wood until she was able to free her right hand. Then she slumped back, clutching her injured fingers to her chest as she watched the water below the dock froth while the grey-eyed man fought for his life.

She finally let herself rest as the exhaustion from the stress and sleepless night crashed over her. Rain dripped from her drenched hair and ran down her face as she leaned against the boat's side. She focussed on breathing, drawing ragged breaths into her aching lungs, until the frantic, churning of the water subsided.

The waves spent themselves on the shore, and at last, the lake was still again, save for the multitude of tiny ripples created by the rain. Sam shivered. She couldn't see any sign of the man or the bodies that had claimed him. Except for the hole in the dock and her aching fingers, it was almost as though the last half hour had never happened. Sam let her eyes close.

She didn't know how long she stayed there, shivering and nursing her throbbing hand, but the rain had eased to a drizzle when something nudged the canoe. Sam jolted to alertness and grabbed at the boat's side, afraid she might be thrown out, but the motion was gentle. The canoe slid across the water, towards the shore, until its base ground to a halt in the dirt. Sam craned her neck to look over both sides of the boat, but couldn't see anything in the murky water.

She was freezing; the rain had sapped all of the warmth from her body. She pushed herself to her feet and stumbled out of the boat, willing her shaking legs to take her weight.

The surrounding forest seemed alive in a way she'd never seen it before, as though the rain had woken a multitude of hibernating beasts. Birds chattered amongst themselves, and farther up the mountain a wild animal called out. Sam stood on the shore for a moment, uncertain about what she should do, and where she should go.

"Sam." The voice was raspy and faint, as though its owner was speaking through a damaged larynx. Sam turned and saw the corpse, her companion for the last three days, standing half a dozen paces behind her. The hollows where his eyes belonged watched her carefully, and he seemed to have posed himself to look as unthreatening as possible.

Sam let her eyes rove over him, taking in the tattered hiking clothes, the shoulder-length bronze hair, and the skin that she thought must have been pale even before his death. She took a half step towards him. "Ian? Ian McKeller?"

The cadaver's cracked lips twitched into a smile, and he gave a small nod, then held his closed fist towards her. "We found these in his pocket."

Sam held out her hand, and Ian dropped the ranger's car keys into it. His fingers, clammy and spongy, brushed her hand, but Sam found it less repulsive than she'd expected. She swallowed thickly as she stared at the keys. "Thank you. For saving me. For everything."

Ian turned his sightless eyes towards the car. "The ranger is still alive, but not for much longer. I treated the wound as well as I could, but... it's becoming harder to remember… who I used to be… what I used to know…" He exhaled a lungful of sticky, moist air and shook his head. "You'll need to hurry, Sam."

"Okay." Sam took a step backwards but couldn't bring herself to turn away. "I'll make sure your… your body is found. And the others. You'll have a proper burial."

Another smile fluttered across the corpse's face, peeling up the edges of the decayed skin on his cheeks. "You know, all of that becomes surprisingly unimportant when you're dead. But I would be grateful if my family knew what happened."

"Of course. I'll make sure."

"And you're welcome to use the paintings. They're as much yours as they are mine."

Her drained mind couldn't understand what he meant, but she nodded anyway.

The corpse gave her a final, gentle smile. "Goodbye, Sam."

The rain had settled to infrequent spits, but it was still enough to make Sam shiver as Ian turned and started towards the lake. She stared at the car keys in her hand, blinking back tears, then drew a shuddering breath as Ian's words filtered through to her. *Brandon's still alive.*

She ran to the car. Brandon had been moved to the passenger seat and leant against the door. Ian had cut off Brandon's shirt and turned it into bandages, which had been wrapped around his torso. Sam held a shaking hand in front of his open mouth and felt his breath—weak but enduring—on her fingertips. She slid into the driver's seat, buckled the belt, and put the keys into the ignition. As the car's motor roared to life, she glanced back at the lake.

Sunlight had broken through the rainclouds and painted large golden streaks across the water's surface. The cabin, beautiful and rustic, was as much a part of the lake as the rocks. It watched over its surroundings. Ian knelt on the dock's edge, in his familiar crouched pose. He turned towards Sam and raised a hand in farewell. Sam returned the gesture, and the corpse slid forward, over the edge of the dock, to plunge into the water.

CHAPTER 19

When arranged in order, the paintings had a startling impact. They started with brief glimpses of the man moving like a wraith through the trees, then focussed on his face and his harsh grey eyes. From there, the paintings moved on to show his victims fighting for their lives, and ultimately losing. The finger was cut off. Then the bodies were thrown off the dock, plunging below the lake's surface, where they would become tangled in weeds and consumed by fish and insects. The narrative was brutal and shocking, but it also held something of a distorted elegance: man pitted against man in nature's arena.

Sam stood with her back to a pillar near the centre of the spacious, well-lit room, her right hand discreetly held behind her back so that the splint wouldn't be too obvious. The grey-eyed man's grappling hook had broken two of her fingers. Looking at the paintings, though, Sam could only feel grateful for how lightly she'd escaped.

The Heritage's patrons walked through the display, murmuring to one another. Occasionally, one would approach her, shake her hand, and congratulate her on the exhibition. They used words such as *impactful* and *mesmerising*, and she received at least three requests for her business card from other gallery owners and art critics.

Brandon inclined his head towards her and murmured into her ear, "They love it."

Sam could only manage a weak, choked chuckle. It still felt unreal to her; in the eight days following her escape from the lake, she'd spent half of her time in the hospital and the other half assisting the police in their investigation. Even though the paintings had been returned to her a few days after she'd arrived home, she'd barely had a chance to look at them, let alone think about them.

She hadn't made the decision to exhibit the paintings lightly. They depicted real events, from memories of a real life that had been lost. But Ian

McKeller's blessing had been the deciding factor. *"You're welcome to use the paintings. They're as much yours as they are mine."*

Brandon casually bumped the back of his right hand into her left, and Sam felt a smile grow over her face as their fingers entwined.

Following their escape, she'd visited the ranger in hospital and celebrated the small triumphs with him as he was moved from ICU to the general ward then finally discharged. Following that, they'd worked together to help the police find the grey-eyed man's cabin. Sam only had a vague idea of where it had been, but Brandon was familiar with the mountain's landscape, and together, they'd been able to pin down the approximate location.

She'd found herself gravitating towards the ranger and his unassuming, steady kindness. His shy invitation for a date couldn't have come soon enough.

Sam was slowly learning to trust him in a way she hadn't trusted anyone since her mother's passing. When she'd told him about the cadaver who had guided her dreams and saved both of their lives, he hadn't scoffed or laughed like she'd been afraid he would, but accepted it with a quiet "wow."

She'd been much more selective about what she'd shared with the police. Instead of telling them the grey-eyed man had been dragged into the lake, she said he'd fallen through the rotten wood. Everyone seemed content with that explanation; when his corpse was fished out of the lake, he'd had lacerations across his body and a substantial head wound. The coroner's report said he'd hit his head while falling through the hole, and drowned.

It had taken some time to discover his name. In the end, Uncle Earnest's guess had been half-right: although he was very much a human, the man was Michael Paluhik. He belonged to the trio of hikers to first disappear around the lake, and his body had, obviously, never been recovered

Friends had described Michael as quiet and shy, but his diary, a tattered book found on one of his cabin's shelves, painted a very different picture. He'd grown up with impulses that he hadn't understood and had struggled to contain. His diary talked about wanting to kill his mother, his siblings, and even his friends. The entries went into increasingly graphic detail about the ways he would do it, the expressions he could picture on their faces, and how he imagined their blood would taste.

He'd managed to control his urges until that fateful backpacking trip with his two closest friends. In the privacy of the woods, he'd murdered them both with his camping knife and dragged their bodies off the path so that the deaths would seem accidental when they were found. He'd taken a single memento from each body: their index fingers.

Knowing that his crimes would be uncovered if he returned to civilisation, Michael built himself a life inside the forest. He knew enough about wilderness survival to live off the land and find clean water, and he occasionally took the two-day hike to the nearest town to purchase anything he wasn't able to build for himself.

According to his diary, the impulses had grown stronger with each passing year. At first, he'd only taken one or two lives a year, choosing from amongst the hikers he'd watched on Trail T1, which ran near his cabin and he considered his domain. But eventually, the cravings had grown so severe that he'd started killing every few months.

Sam would have been his nineteenth victim in eight years.

She still couldn't understand how or why Ian and his companions had retained their autonomy after death. She and Brandon had bandied theories back and forth; Brandon had found an outdated webpage that talked about Harob Lake being home to otherworldly spirits, and thought that some sort of energy had sustained the victims' awareness. Sam thought Ian, the last hiker to go missing, might have had some sort of spiritual aptitude, and his death had been the catalyst for its unleashing and had, in turn, woken the other bodies.

Either way, they owed Ian their lives. His funeral

was scheduled for the following morning. Because they'd worked so closely with the police to retrieve his body, both Sam and Brandon had received an invitation to attend.

Even though the dead man didn't have a high opinion of funerals, Sam was looking forward to seeing him finally laid to rest. She'd ordered a special bunch of liriope flowers, which had grown in abundance in the lake he had become so fond of.

Sam leaned her head against Brandon's shoulder and felt her smile widen as he gently squeezed her hand in response.

the
end

ABOUT THE AUTHOR

Darcy Coates has always loved horror. She's especially fond of hauntings, monsters, and creatures without names.

She came first place in the Hpathy Short Story Competition (2013) for The Passing Hour, and first place in the Wyong Short Story Competition (2013, Adult Division), for The Mallory Haunting.

also by
DARCY COATES

GHOST CAMERA
(a haunting novella)

THE HAUNTING *of* GILLESPIE HOUSE
(a haunted house novel)

THE HAUNTING *of* BLACKWOOD HOUSE
(a haunted house novel)

QUARTER *to* MIDNIGHT
(fifteen tales of horror and suspense)

BITES
(3-minute horror series)

HOUSE *of* SHADOWS
(a gothic romance)

Find these stories and more at:
www.amazon.com/author/darcycoates

Subscribe for author updates:
http://bit.ly/1PeXrpI

76736695R00095

Made in the USA
Columbia, SC
09 September 2017